CW01648067

THE DEVIL

&

THE DEPTHS OF MURDER

A DI Lizzie Holland Crime Thriller

SAMANTHA TURNER

FORESHORE
publishing

Published in Great Britain in 2022 by
Foreshore Publishing Ltd
The Forge 397-411
Westferry Road, Isle of Dogs,
London, E14 3AE
Reg. No. 13358650
www.foreshorepublishing.com

The home of quality short fiction.

Set in Garamond Pro
Typeset by Deepak Gupta
Printed and bound in Great Britain by 4Edge Ltd, Essex.

Copyright © Samantha Turner 2023
The moral right of the author has been asserted.

This book is sold subject to the condition that it shall not, by way of trade or otherwise, be lent, re-sold, hired out, or otherwise circulated without the publisher's prior consent in any form of binding or cover other than that in which it is published and without a similar condition, including this condition, being imposed on the subsequent purchaser.

This is a work of fiction. Any names or characters, businesses or places, events, or incidents, are fictitious. Any resemblance to actual persons, living or dead, or actual events is purely coincidental.

ISBN 978-1-7395930-9-4

Forward

My love affair with words began at a very young age. I have always loved nothing more than to disappear into the world of a wonderful book. It is by far my favourite form of escapism. For many years, I have dabbled with writing and have been heavy with a longing to create my own books. However, my life at the time left me with very little time and energy to create. Fast forward to 2020 when I decided to make the terrifying and exhilarating decision to step with both feet into my dream job as a writer. Lizzie Holland is the person I always wanted to be, a character brave enough to take a chance on a new life. Also, through Lizzie, I face my worst fears, but she has the strength to turn tragedy into something positive. Lizzie is the brave, strong, exceptional woman who hides deep inside my own insecure heart.

(*Samantha Turner, 2022*).

The Devil You Know

1

THE BLINDING GLARE OF the fluorescent tubing lights was giving Lizzie a headache again. The constant flickering plus the annoying tinny, tapping sound made her want to smash the damned thing. Not a good idea as the glass can splinter and blind you. After twenty-three years of working here, you would expect her to be used to those horrible lights. You would also think someone would be sent from head office to change the bulb, but no. Not until they were working by candlelight would anything be fixed in this box of doom.

The box of doom, that is what Lizzie liked to call the pharmacy where she had spent the best years of her life. A flat-roofed, glass-fronted tiny little building on the corner of a council estate, roasting hot in the summer and cold in the winter. Having left community high school with average GCSE results and no clue as to what to do next, Lizzie's mum scoured the local job pages until she found a suitable position for her youngest daughter. The job was exciting when Elizabeth first started at the pharmacy, dispensing medicines that she had never even heard of, serving customers, and learning about how different drugs acted on the body. Not working was never an option in the Evans' household. As a working-class family living in the North West, they did not have much money. Both Lizzie and her elder sister Amber had been expected to find a job as soon as they left school. Although her parents worked full time in the local factory life was a struggle financially. College and university were never an option. Get a job and earn your keep, simple as that. There was no money for airy-fairy dreams or ambition. So, Groundhog Day it was for Lizzie. Five days a week, the same people, the same place, the exact same routine. For twenty-three long years.

Outside of the box of doom, life inevitably happened. Girly holidays abroad and nights out at the clubs in town, doing what most young people Lizzie's age were doing. One warm night in May while out with friends, Lizzie met a local lad called David Holland. He was four years older with blonde hair and deep brown eyes; they hit it off immediately and soon became inseparable. Lizzie's parents got on well with David and vice versa. After a long engagement, Lizzie and David were married in a small ceremony and moved into a modest house on the outskirts of town. David also worked in a factory, and it was hard graft for the minimum wage, but he never complained and compared to his days in the army this job was easy. Although they never had any children or lots of money, Lizzie and David were happy and very much in love. Lizzie had her hiking and David had his politics. He was very opinionated and liked to argue about controversial subjects online. These heated discussions kept him occupied. The only thing spoiling Lizzie's contentment was her job in the pharmacy. It was a stressful occupation with not enough staff to cover the workload, and the insidious dread had been creeping up inside her for years, causing anxiety and panic attacks. 'There has to be more to life than this', Lizzie would whine repeatedly. She wanted to be inspired to use her creativity, but no one wanted to know. She was dreaming, her family said, and everyone hates their job. You just get on with it. Better the devil you know blah blah blah and Lizzie was sick of hearing it. The Evans family do not take risks, do not like change. 'Ambition isn't for people like us', they said.

After many months of pondering and battling self-doubt, Lizzie decided she was going to leap. She would leave her safe, familiar job, ignore the prophets of doom in her ear, and risk making a fool of herself in the hope of breaking free. Now all she had to do was pluck up the courage to tell everyone and brace herself for the onslaught of negativity.

If Lizzie had been the kind of person to give in to pressure and doubt, then maybe she would have listened to her parents and her sister when they told her she was being ridiculous and having a mid-life crisis. Lizzie however, was stubborn, and had made up her mind. It wasn't a decision she had made lightly, and she and David had discussed it at length. He wasn't over the moon about it, but he was willing to support her as he had seen how the job had been affecting Lizzie's mental health lately. With nervous excitement and a little sadness, Lizzie gave in her notice at the pharmacy. Saying a teary goodbye to colleagues and customers who had also become friends over the years, she walked out of the doom box for the final time. Lizzie would kind of miss the old place; it had been a big part of her life since she was a teenager, and many of the customers had watched her grow up. Now was the time to move on, though. The time for a new adventure had arrived.

2

LIZZIE WAS NOT GOING to spend the next twenty-five years in another humdrum job that she would hate. After searching the internet, she came across a fully funded NVQ 3 college course to become a nail technician, to learn how to apply all kinds of artificial nails and designs. This course was perfect! It was creative and could lead to Lizzie having her own mobile business one day. By advertising on social media, posting leaflets through doors, and promoting special offers, she could become a success. This course could be just the thing she had been hoping to find.

After sixteen weeks, the nail technician course was complete, and Lizzie was eager to go with her new business venture. Instagram, Facebook, and local advertising had given her a regular client base, and Lizzie enjoyed the interaction with new people. Armed with her satellite navigation and her box of tricks, she would drive to the house of the client to create all kinds of fabulous false nails.

Lizzie was always a little apprehensive before going to a new client's house for the first time, but they were very welcoming and offered her a coffee. On that particular morning, though, after receiving a message on her Facebook business page to go to the house of seventeen-year-old Leanne Parker, Lizzie's nerves were a little more profound than usual. She could not say why. Leanne seemed friendly enough, and her online profile was the kind you would expect. There was just something unnerving Lizzie, maybe because the address was a bit secluded. No, she was being silly, and the old anxiety was just popping up today. Her business was important, and she could not afford to turn down a perfectly good client on a wobble of nerves.

3

ROY PETERS CURSED AS his internet connection crashed again. The signal in this countryside area was crap, and the Wi-Fi was virtually non-existent. After turning everything off at the wall and waiting for thirty seconds, thankfully it seemed to be up and running again. Eagerly he logged back on to his Facebook account and began scrolling through the newsfeed. Roy had lived alone since his elderly parents passed away. With no siblings, the run- down cottage and surrounding two-acre garden belonged to him. Not short of money, Roy had been left a substantial inheritance but had no interest in spending it on the house.

Facebook was almost like having friends and kept Roy company in his secluded existence. He could be anyone he wanted online, and no one would ever know who the real person behind the keyboard was. Of course, Roy did not have any friends, online or otherwise. He had always been a bit different, odd some might say. As a child, the nasty little boy liked to keep insects in jars and watch them struggle frantically to escape until finally, the air ran out, and they lost the fight and died. It excited him that he had power over their fate.

As a keen hunter, Roy often went out at night with his shotgun. The area was abundant with wild deer and rabbits, foxes, and pheasants. Although he enjoyed the thrill of stalking the animals, for Roy, it was all over too quickly: bang, one shot, and the animal was dead. He had needed more and more kills to keep up the excitement. Maturing into adulthood saw him discover the dark side of the internet, where Roy Peters moved on to a more sinister form of entertainment. He fed his evil desires by watching violent snuff videos where victims are tortured and murdered on camera. Roy was a virgin, too shy to approach a woman, too weird for any woman to approach him: so, these vile recordings aroused the dominating sexual part of his sick personality.

Living alone in the Lancashire countryside, no one could know what Roy was planning in that sick mind of his. The internet was not enough. He wanted a real person in this house. The very thought of them vulnerable and alone, wide- eyed, and frightened in his control made him dizzy with anticipation.

4

LIZZIE'S RELIABLE LITTLE FIAT bumped along the rough country lane as she tried to avoid the many potholes. This house certainly was out of the way. Green fields and hills stretched out on either side, the sky dark with threatening clouds on the horizon. A posh robotic voice told her she was just three minutes away from reaching her destination. Thank the Lord she thought; it had not been an easy place to find despite the sat nav, and Lizzie was more than ready for a coffee and the bathroom. Rowan Cottage finally came into view, and Lizzie could see the old place had not been modernised.

The lone cottage built of grey stone had a traditional wooden front door and a brass letterbox. The door had once been a pretty, red colour, but now only faded bits of peeling paint remained. The four windows also had wooden frames that were damp and crumbling, the glass all dirty and old. This wreck of a house was not the kind of place she would expect a young, image-conscious girl to live. But who was Lizzie to judge? Maybe Leanne's parents did not have much money, or the house was nicer inside. It wasn't any of her business.

Taking her box of supplies out of the car boot, Lizzie made her way to the front door of the cottage and knocked firmly. Looking around her, she could see a large garden full of nettles and prickles. If they were not going to mow it, maybe they could scatter wildflower seeds, she thought.

The sudden creak of the door brought Lizzie back to the moment. In front of her stood a balding, chubby man about fifty-odd years old wearing brown cord trousers and a bobbly green jumper. His skin looked pale and sallow with eyes small and beady like a snake.

'Hello', said Lizzie. 'I've got an appointment with Leanne Parker; I hope I have the right address'.

5

AMBER EVANS OPENED HER bleary eyes and tried to focus them on the bedside clock. Seven am.'Urghh', she sighed. Amber was not a morning person. At forty-five, she was four years older than her sister Lizzie. Her auburn hair had started to show signs of grey, and her pale, freckled complexion screamed for more Botox even though no one else seemed to agree. Ageing was not going to stop Amber looking her best, if only she could afford the expensive treatments. Working as a shop assistant would never make her a millionaire, to be quite honest she didn't want to work at all. Amber wanted to be a lady of leisure with a wealthy husband and his limitless credit card in her purse.

As children, Amber and Lizzie would have vicious cat fights, tearing out fists of hair before their Mum or Dad pulled them apart. As they grew up though, Lizzie and Amber became best friends, so Amber felt a little lost when David turned up. He was a nice lad who adored Lizzie, but Amber could not help feeling a bit resentful. Amber had not been lucky in love; she was quite fussy, and no one seemed to meet her high expectations. After a few failed relationships, she had given up looking for Mr Right. When Lizzie and David got married, it was like a kick in the teeth. Amber was the eldest; it should have been her.

The years passed, and Amber would often meet Lizzie for coffee and lunch. They would visit each other's houses and spend time together with their parents. It was never long before the conversation turned to both sisters complaining about work. Amber may not have the same stress that Lizzie had, but working at the DIY store was boring. The only benefit was the discount on paint and wallpaper. Lately though, Lizzie had begun to get on Amber's nerves; maybe it was the antidepressants she was taking, but Lizzie had suddenly become all positive and hopeful. Amber used to like the fact that they both hated their jobs: it gave her comfort that Lizzie was just as unhappy and negative. There was camaraderie in their despair. Now Lizzie was spouting all kinds of rubbish, 'anything is possible'. 'Be thankful for what you have'. 'It's never too late to change your life'. Yea right. She was on another planet!

Lizzie did change her life though, and surprise surprise, everything landed on her lap as usual. Now a qualified nail technician, she chose her hours and was making a steady income faffing around doing arty nails and drinking coffee all day. It was alright for some! Knowing Lizzie, she would end up with a salon, become rich, and get all the things that Amber wanted. It wasn't fair at all.

6

HEARING A KNOCK ON the front door, Roy peered through the yellowing net curtain and saw a red Fiat Punto parked up outside; this must be her. His palms started to sweat, and he had to compose himself before answering the door. 'Stay calm', he told himself. 'Everything is in place: this is what you wanted'. Roy opened the door and saw the woman that he had been secretly stalking via Facebook for the last four weeks. Lizzie Holland was pretty and didn't look her age; her ample breasts stood out against her small, slightly chubby stature and large hazel eyes made her appear innocent like a doe. She wore a plain white t-shirt and fitted blue jeans that clung perfectly to her wide hips. Pushing a strand of long brown hair from her face Lizzie smiled and introduced herself.

'Oh, yes, of course, please come inside', said Roy.

The first thing that Lizzie noticed when entering the run- down cottage was the smell – old fashioned and musty due to the damp and black mould that was visible around the windows and in the corner of the walls. The carpet that ran through the living room and up the stairs was brown with yellow patterns, threadbare in places, and looked like it needed a thorough vacuuming. There was a shabby beige sofa positioned in front of a real fire and an old-fashioned rocking chair in the corner. A mahogany side table stood next to it with a tassel shaded lamp. There were no family photographs at all. Not even one, which seemed odd to her for a man who had a teenage daughter. Everything about the room was old except the television and Skybox.

'My daughter Leanne is on her way home from college; she has a half-day today but is running a bit late. I'm sure she won't be too long; can I make you a drink while you wait?' Roy asked in a softly spoken voice.

'A black coffee, no sugar would be lovely thanks'. 'Would it be alright if I used your bathroom first, though? It was quite a drive to find you'.

'Up the stairs, along the landing and it's the door at the bottom', Roy replied.

This was going to be even better than he anticipated. He could quickly drop the Rohypnol drug into the coffee without the risk of being detected.

On entering the bathroom, a nauseating green suite greeted Lizzie, limescale in abundance.

'Let's get this over with', she thought.

Making her way back down the stairs, Lizzie hoped there would be a table of some sort where she would be able to work. She would need space to set up all the nail equipment for Leanne. The aroma of strong coffee hit her nostrils as Lizzie re-entered the living room where a surprisingly clean cup was handed to her.

'Thank you; sorry, I don't know your name'.

'Roy, I'm Roy, Leanne's Dad. She won't be much longer'.

The ticking antique clock on the mantelpiece only added to the uncomfortable silence. Two thirty-one pm; she would wait until three, and if Leanne was not here by then, she would make her excuses and leave. This cottage was giving her the creeps, and there was something a bit off about Roy; he kept staring at her and asking if her coffee was strong enough. He was making Lizzie feel awkward and self-conscious.

7

TEN PM. FINALLY, DAVID'S shift was over. It had been a busy eight hours at the factory, and he had needed to fix a few problems with the machines, causing even his well-built arms to ache a little. Not to worry, soon he would be home. Lizzie will have a freshly brewed coffee and a cuddle waiting. Lizzie would usually text David about six o'clock when she knew he would be on his tea break, but he had not heard from her tonight. She must have had a late client or something.

As he turned the key in the white PVC door to their home, David walked into a silent and dark living room. No coffee. No Lizzie. This behaviour was strange and out of character for her. He turned on the lights and walked around the house, searching each room and calling Lizzie's name. David checked the garage and saw that her car wasn't there. Taking his mobile phone from his pocket, he dialled Lizzie's number only to be answered by her voicemail. A slight panic was growing in his stomach now, but David tried to keep calm and rational. Sitting down on the cream suede sofa, he phoned Lizzie's Mum, then her sister, and then her two best friends, but they hadn't heard from her either. He felt bad for worrying them, but he had to find out where Lizzie could be. The police would not do anything yet as it was too soon to file a missing person report. A thought occurred to David, Facebook. He would check when Lizzie had last been active on her page and check her business account for any client appointments. Maybe she had rushed off and not had time to charge her phone or the car had broken down somewhere. Nine hours ago, Lizzie had not been active on Facebook for nine hours. That was worrying, but if her mobile had died then, of course, she could not access her account. Still, nine hours was a long time for Lizzie to be out even if David was right about the car.

On Lizzie's business account, David could see a list of clients she had booked in today. The last one had been to a Leanne Parker of Rowen Cottage, Brierley Lane, at two pm. Brierley Lane; David had not heard of it and used Google maps to look it up. It was about a twelve-mile drive out into the country, off the beaten track with rough scrubland and not much else nearby.

There was a telephone number for the client, so despite the late hour, David decided to give her a call to make sure Lizzie had made it to her house that afternoon. The line rang out; maybe she was in bed by now. Taking in a deep breath to calm him, David walked to the mirror. His tired eyes showed signs of stress and worry. The speckles of grey in his close-cropped hair would turn white if Lizzie didn't come home soon.

8

LIZZIE HOLLAND LAY LIKE A sack of potatoes in the corner of the sofa. Roy feared that he had not given her enough of the drug. Minutes had felt like hours as he had nervously waited for the Rohypnol to take effect. It was once Lizzie had tried to stand up that she had been overcome by light-headedness and had fallen backwards onto the cushions. She had mumbled something and then swiftly fallen unconscious. Roy knew that he had to act fast. It would not be long before someone noticed that Lizzie had not arrived home. A rush of fear and excitement surged through his veins. Taking the corners of the large polyester throw that draped over the sofa, Roy wrapped Lizzie inside it. Dragging her body down into the dimly lit cellar, he carefully unwrapped Lizzie from the throw and took a moment to look at his victim. Like Snow White Lizzie was quite beautiful in sleep, and Roy could not resist leaning down to run his bitten fingernail over her cheek. Her skin was soft and plump, with a little flush of pink here and there. He had better get on with things; Prince Charming would be here soon enough.

Roy had been carefully planning this day for weeks. How he would trick Lizzie into the house and what the best sedative would be. Setting up the fake Facebook profile had been genius. He could not believe how easy it had been and how quick people were to accept a friend request from a stranger. Glancing around the dusty cellar, Roy checked that all his tools were close to hand. A trip to the DIY store had been enough to buy what he needed: cable ties, clear plastic bags, and some rope twine. The red headed shop assistant had been very helpful. The cold, grey stone walls of the cellar were thick enough to block out any noise although there were not any neighbours for miles.

Walking back over to where Lizzie's unconscious body lay, Roy rolled her onto her front and removed her white trainers and socks. Immaculate toenails were painted in a deep red to match her fingernails. With the largest of the cable ties, he fastened her ankles together tightly. Next, pulling her arms behind her, he used another cable tie, securing together her small wrists. Roy propped up Lizzie's lolling head onto a piece of foam with a hole in the middle that he had made earlier. He did not want her to suffocate. Not yet.

9

LIZZIE WOKE UP FEELING sickly with the worst headache ever. There was a musty smell and something strange under her face. On opening her eyes and seeing nothing, she could feel that she was lying face down on the floor. Disorientated and fuzzy, Lizzie tried to move, causing searing pain to shoot through her already aching body. Her wrists and ankles were stinging, and panic surged in her heart as the reality dawned on her. She was tied up and could not move. Lizzie's breath quickened, and the rising dread rose like a wave as the familiar panic attack took over her body and mind. Breaking into a cold sweat, her body began to tremble. Frantically wriggling and trying to ignore the agony of the plastic ties cutting into her skin, she managed to roll herself onto her back. The room was in darkness, and the floor was cold even though she seemed to be lying on a thin blanket of some sort.

'Focus. Count to ten. Breathe. In and out, in and out'. Lizzie tried to calm herself. Her memory was blank, and she just couldn't remember how she had gotten there.

Panic began to rise once more, but Lizzie knew that if she was going to escape, then she must remain calm. Lizzie was going to get out of there. That was the one truth that she did know. 'If some madman thinks I am going to die here in this black hovel, leaving my beloved David alone, then he is sadly mistaken'. She told herself with conviction.

Lizzie was fully clothed apart from her bare feet. Instinctively she felt that she had not been sexually assaulted, but who knew what this crazy person or people had in store for her? They could come back at any moment; Lizzie had to do something and fast. Her eyes adjusted to the darkness, and she could just about make out a few unfamiliar shapes. The room she was in was cold, and as she shuffled her stiff body along the floor, she hit what felt like the bottom of a flight of stone steps.

'Where in hell am I?' she asked the darkness.

'You are in my cellar'. The voice that came out of nowhere made Lizzie scream, and her body convulse. Roy Peters was sitting in the far corner of the cellar wearing night-vision goggles. He had been patiently waiting for Lizzie to wake up. Watching her squirm and panic in her incapacitated state had given him great enjoyment. He was surprised that she had managed to wriggle to the bottom of the stairs all tied up as she was. Lizzie was a fighter. This was going to be fun.

Footsteps in the dark walked towards Lizzie. With sweaty hands around her arms, she was dragged away from the stairs. Heavy breathing and stale whiskey on his breath, her captor pushed Lizzie face down onto her front once more. Lizzie began to scream and struggle, tears of fear, anger, and frustration pouring down her face.

'Let me go! Please don't do this', Lizzie begged. 'I have a family; I have a life'.

The room lit up, and Lizzie screwed her eyes tight shut against the shock of the sudden brightness. Slowly she opened them again and tentatively lifted her head off the floor.

Before Lizzie could focus on her surroundings, all the air was suddenly stolen from her lungs as a plastic bag was put over her head and pulled tight across her face. Terror like she had never known gripped her entire being as Lizzie fought for air. Sucking in nothing but plastic through her nose and mouth, her eyes began to bulge, her lungs were on fire, and her body jerked. This was it, the end of her. Nothing had prepared Lizzie for the nightmare of what was happening. No matter how many horror movies she had watched and screamed at the victim to fight harder, when it was happening to you, it was all futile. Lizzie was alone in a cellar with a psychopath, and no one was there to save her.

As Lizzie began to descend into blackness, and her last breath was about to leave her body, the plastic bag was quickly ripped from her head. Lizzie deeply gulped in the beautiful air as it re-inflated her desperate lungs and she began to cough violently.

Repeatedly, Roy tortured Lizzie until she was utterly exhausted and on the brink of death. When Lizzie was just about to give up, the cellar suddenly returned to darkness and footsteps up the stairs meant she was alone.

A while later, Lizzie had recovered enough to be aware of warm dampness down below. She had wet herself, and the smell of urine strangely made her realise that she was thirsty.

10

DRIVING DOWN THE BUMPY track towards Rowan Cottage, David Holland scanned the darkness for any sign of Lizzie or her car. This area was a lonely place with no other houses for miles. Just pitch blackness in every direction. The glare of the car headlights on full beam fell upon a red shape up ahead. As David got closer, he could see that it was a red car. Lizzie's car, parked in front of a slightly dilapidated cottage. Bringing his vehicle to a halt, David ran over to the red Fiat. Peering inside, he realised he had left his head torch in the glovebox. Once he had retrieved it, he could see that the car was empty, and the doors were locked.

'Why would the car still be here?' David whispered. Surely, she wouldn't have tried to walk home. Something was very wrong; he could feel it in his gut. Lizzie was still here somewhere.

Music broke the silence and made David jump. 'The self- preservation society' rang out from the mobile phone in his pocket. It was Amber, Lizzie's sister.

'Have you found her. Is she home?' the anxious voice asked. 'We are all out of our mind with worry here. Mum and Dad want to phone the police, but I've persuaded them to wait until we heard from you'.

David explained where he was and told Amber to stay calm. He would speak to the people who live in the cottage and ring Amber back with any news.

Rowan Cottage was in complete darkness, but as it was one- thirty in the morning, he was not surprised. Making his way to the window, David tried to peer inside, but the grubby net curtains obscured his already limited view. Knocking on the door seemed wrong and intrusive at this hour, but his missing wife's car was parked outside of this house, and David wanted answers.

After knocking and waiting, knocking, and listening, David was growing impatient. He walked through the overgrown garden, thankful that he was still wearing his thick polyester work trousers and steel toe capped boots. Around the back of the cottage was another dense patch of land. His head torch shone on a set of stairs that seemed to lead down to a lower part of the cottage.

Despite the torch, David found it difficult to navigate his way through the triffid-like nettles and prickles. What felt like broken bits of brick or stone was buried amongst the long grass and suddenly David tripped over. Landing heavily onto the jungle-like ground, his head torch hit a piece of sharp brick, and the light went out. 'Shit', cursed David as he struggled to pick himself up, his hands and face stinging from nettle stings and scratches.

It took some minutes for his eyes to adjust to the dark, but eventually, he could see the steps once more. Taking more care this time, he walked over to them and descended until he reached a steel door. There was no window, and the door had been locked from the inside. David banged furiously on the door and then placed his ear against the cold hard steel. Nothing. He could not hear anything but the sound of his own rapid breathing.

11

ROY STEADIED HIMSELF AGAINST the kitchen counter, the whiskey glass in his hand shook as adrenaline coursed through his body. Just knowing that Lizzie was still down in the cellar, frightened and in his total control was thrilling. When he had slipped the bag over her head, it had been such a shock to Lizzie. Oh, how she had gasped and panicked, writhed like a fox in a trap. Those beautiful eyes, begging for life, and only he could give it or take it away. Like God, he would decide the moment of her death.

Lizzie had lost control of her bladder during the ordeal; the fear he had instilled in her excited him further. He would clean her up, give her a drink of water, and then leave her to calm down a bit. Then he would use the rope.

Rummaging through his mum's old clothes, Roy found a blue flowery skirt with an elasticated waistband. It would do. If Lizzie wet herself again, at least most of it would just end up on the floor. He could just strip her naked, but it was cold down there, and he didn't want her getting hypothermia and losing consciousness on him. Where would be the fun in that? He had no real desire to have sex with Lizzie either; it was the thrill of having control and inflicting suffering that aroused him.

With the skirt in one hand and a plastic cup of water in the other, Roy made his way back down the cellar stairs. Lizzie was still face down on the ground, shaking and sobbing. On hearing Roy's approach, she began to groan and roll about on the floor. Roy pulled her up into a sitting position against the cobwebbed wall.

Her swollen and red eyes glared at him. Taking a knife, he cut the ties that bound Lizzie's ankles together and then began to unzip her jeans. She shouted and pleaded for him to stop. He peeled her soiled underwear and jeans down her chubby thighs.

'Don't worry, Lizzie; I'm not going to rape you. That isn't why you're here'.

After slipping the skirt up onto her waist, he fastened new plastic ties around her ankles. Holding the cup of water to her lips, Roy could see Lizzie was afraid to drink. Her thirst soon overtook suspicion, and she greedily gulped down the water.

'Who are you? Why are you doing this to me?' Lizzie must have been feeling brave, he thought.

'I'm Roy, don't you remember Lizzie? All will be revealed in good time'.

Leaving Lizzie in the sitting position, he walked back up the cellar stairs and turned off the light. Just as he was about to walk away, Roy heard a loud banging on the outer door of the cellar that led into the back garden. He was here. He had found them. Roy knew that he would; he had counted on it.

12

DAVID HAD JUST ABOUT RUN out of patience. Fighting his way back to the front of the cottage, he redialled the number that he had for Leanne Parker. From inside the house, he heard the bell-like sound of a telephone. No one came to answer it. No shadows passed the window, and no lights were switched on. Not knowing what to do next, David returned to his car and dialled 999. After answering a range of frustrating and pointless questions, he was informed that a couple of police officers would be sent to his location. David was told to wait in the car, and under no circumstances was he to attempt entry into the cottage.

Waiting for the police to arrive was torture. Lizzie was in that house, and God only knew what was happening to her. Maybe she was hurt or dead. David's mind was spinning with worst-case scenarios.

Checking the time on his phone, he saw that it was two-twenty-seven am.

'What is taking the police so long? I've had enough of this shit', he said aloud. Opening the boot of his car, he pulled out a four-inch serrated fishing knife and marched determinedly over to the cottage. In a state of desperation, David tried the handle on the front door; to his surprise the door was unlocked. Using every inch of his old army training, David crept stealthily through the door and felt his way into the cottage. Every fibre of his body was tense and his senses on high alert. Fumbling around the walls with one hand, he found a light switch and flicked it downwards. Nothing happened. The cottage remained in blackness. If only the damned head torch hadn't broken.

Another idea immediately burst into David's mind. He would turn his car to face the windows and shine the headlights into the cottage. Retracing his steps, David could see the open front door, but before he could reach it, something hard hit the back of his head. Reaching up to touch the pain, David felt a warm liquid trickle through his fingers. Turning around, he saw what he could only describe as a dark figure with weirdly shaped eyes.

'Hello, David', said the figure. 'I've been expecting you'.

Bewildered and woozy David opened his mouth to speak, but another blow to the head knocked him cold to the floor along with his knife.

Returning the iron poker to the fireside, Roy sat on the sofa feeling rather pleased with himself. Snow White was in the cellar, and Prince Charming lay bleeding at his feet. Who would have thought it? Soft little Roy who everyone thought was pathetic had outsmarted an ex-army man.

'Not so tough now, are you David?' Scoffed Roy smugly. He would switch the electric back on and let David see just what 'fuckwit' Roy was capable of.

Onto a wooden chair brought in from the kitchen, Roy heaved up David's limp body. David was heavy, and Roy had to catch his breath before tying him to the chair with rope twine. He looked in a bad way. The blood was dripping in a line down his forehead, but he was still breathing. Roy would wake him up soon and then the real fun could begin. As soon as Roy had realised that David Holland had arrived at the cottage, it was time to put his cruel plan into action.

Turning off the electric and donning his night-vision goggles, he had lain in wait for David to enter.

Now it was time to fetch precious little Lizzie to play the game called 'who will survive the longest?'

Lizzie heard the door at the top of the stairs open and began screaming and begging as Roy and his retro brown cords plodded towards her. At that moment, a fragment of memory flashed into her brain: the client: the creepy cottage: Roy. 'Oh my God!' Lizzie cried.

'Oh Lizzie, Lizzie, we're going to have some fun tonight, just the three of us. I just need to take a few bits and pieces upstairs then I'll come back for you'.

Roy's feminine voice sounded almost friendly like he was talking to his mother or someone.

'The three of us'. That was what he had said. 'Oh Lord no, please no'. Lizzie whispered in sheer desperation.

'There's another one up there, another evil bastard waiting to torture me again'.

Gathering more ties, a nail gun, and some plastic bags, Roy made a point of waving them in front of Lizzie as he made his way back up the stairs.

13

A GLARE OF BRIGHTNESS CAUSED David to jerk awake, and for a split second, he didn't know where he was. Throbbing pain in his head and blood on his hands was all it took for him to remember. The light was back on, and David's arms had been tightly tied to the chair that he was uncomfortably sitting on. Instinctively, he began to wriggle his arms from the rope causing his wrists to bleed. He felt sick and light-headed, but David knew he had to get free before that psycho came back. Something terrible had happened to Lizzie. Wherever she was, David had to find her. His beautiful, kind Lizzie; what if she was already dead? What if he was too late? Tears began to blur his eyes. 'No!' He said to himself.

With raging anger, he ignored the pain and furiously pushed his wrists back and forward against the rope, nervously glancing around the room for his attacker returning. A blood-stained iron poker left by an old fireplace caught his eye, and then something silver and shiny sticking up from underneath the sofa. It was the fishing knife! He must have dropped it earlier, and that maniac hadn't noticed.

Managing to semi-stand up while still tied to the chair, David awkwardly lay down on his side close to the blade of the knife and rubbed the rope against the edge. After what felt like an eternity, the rope severed, and he quickly released his other wrist. Picking up the knife, David moved slowly out of the living room and down a long hallway where a heavy-looking door at the end stood slightly ajar. Next to the door, leaning carelessly against the wall David recognised a twelve-gauge shotgun. Inching his way towards it, David caught a glimpse of what was behind the door.

Stone steps led down into what must be the room he had found at the back of the cottage earlier. Lizzie sat against a wall traumatised but alive. Her hands and feet were tied, and she was wearing some old-fashioned flowery skirt. She looked small and terrified; her eyes were bloodshot and swollen. At that moment, David had never felt more in love with Lizzie or more afraid that he could still lose her.

The back of a man suddenly came into view next to Lizzie, and David recognized the smarmy voice of his attacker as Roy taunted her. As quietly as possible, David put the knife in his pocket and picked up the shotgun, relieved to see that it was loaded. Knowing that this was his only chance before the blood loss from his head caused him to pass out again, David kicked back the cellar door and got into position.

The man on the stairs who looked into David's eyes with shock and disbelief was not what David had been expecting. Although the man had spoken softly, David assumed he was a solidly built son of a bitch, not a flabby, ageing mummy's boy, but David wasn't going to underestimate the crazy fucker. Firing the shotgun with precision, he watched as their attacker flew back down the stairs, and his insides gruesomely decorated the cellar walls.

14

DETECTIVE CHIEF INSPECTOR CATHY Wallis sat at her desk and ran nicotine-stained fingers over her tired eyes. It had been a long night, and she was more than ready for her bed, but this paperwork wouldn't write itself. Earlier on there had been a few drunk and disorderly brought into the police station, but other than that, it was relatively calm. She was just about to grab herself another coffee when Sergeant Steve McNairy tapped on her door.

'Have you got a sec Ma'am?' he asked in his now slightly faded Scottish accent.

'What is it, McNairy? It's nearly two am, and I've not even finished this yet'.

'Yes, sorry Ma'am. It's just we've received a call about a missing woman. Her husband got home from work tonight, and she wasn't there'.

'For Christ's sake McNairy, she's probably off with her fancy man. How long has she been missing?'

'Thirteen hours Ma'am, but before you jump in again, the husband has found her abandoned car… outside Rowan Cottage'.

Cathy was suddenly wide awake. Rowan Cottage was the home of Roy Peters, a sad but dangerous little man with a penchant for cruelty and online stalking. He had previously been brought in for questioning over abusive and threatening behaviour on social media but had been released with a caution. Roy remained on their watch list though, as Cathy always believed that he was capable of something more sinister. He already had a juvenile record for killing a school friend's dog. Roy had claimed that the 'friend' had set the dog on him after an argument and that he only strangled the dog in self-defence. An eyewitness told a different story, and Roy was given a ban from keeping animals for ten years.

'Let's go and check it out', said DCI Wallis. 'I've got a bad feeling about this. You can tell me all the details on the way, McNairy'. Two cars had been parked up outside the cottage where Roy Peters lived alone. A red Fiat Punto and a white Nissan Juke. After asking for a vehicle check, it was established by dispatch that both cars belonged to Elizabeth and David Holland.

Sergeant McNairy pulled up behind the Nissan and turned off the engine. Stepping out of the car, they could see that the cottage lights were on, and they could not hear any disturbance from inside.

'Maybe it's a false alarm, Ma'am, or the wife is having it off with Roy'. Steve McNairy was thinking aloud, and DCI Wallis shot him a look of disbelief.

'Have you ever seen Roy Peters?' she asked. 'Elizabeth Holland would have to be blind for a start, and that's before she smelled his breath'.

Sergeant McNairy gave a slight smile behind his substantial brown beard.

A loud and sudden gunshot pierced the early morning silence instantly changing the atmosphere. Cathy's voice was serious.

'That came from inside the cottage'. She immediately radioed for backup.

'This is DCI Cathy Wallis with Sergeant Steve McNairy in attendance at Rowan Cottage, Brierley Lane, in Newsham requesting immediate backup and ambulance. Shots fired; I repeat shots fired at Rowan Cottage. Backup required immediately'.

'Do we go in Ma'am?'

'No, we stay here and wait for backup McNairy. We are unarmed and have no idea what's going on in there'.

15

STAGGERING DOWN TOWARDS HER was the man with the gun. His head was severely bleeding, and he seemed to be shaking. Lizzie began to sob uncontrollably as her bruised and bloodied husband wrapped his arms around her and pulled the fishing knife from his pocket.

'I'm so sorry, Lizzie. I should have found you sooner'.

David's voice was raw with emotion as he cut the plastic ties from her wrists and feet. Immediately Lizzie lifted a painful hand to the cut on his head. Her voice was hoarse.

'You're hurt, David. What did Roy do to you?'

'I'm alright, Lizzie. We need to get out of here. Can you walk?' Lifting her gently up off the floor, David helped his fragile wife to her feet. Lizzie glanced at the lifeless body of her captor as he lay sprawled in a pool of blood.

'What are we going to do, David? You've killed him'.

As if in answer to her question, a police armed response team appeared at the top of the stairs. Lizzie was once again facing the barrel of a gun. Urgent voices shouted a warning for them to stay where they were and to raise their hands above their heads. David turned his face to look at Lizzie one last time, smiled a little, mouthed 'I love you', and then fell heavily to the ground.

Following the armed response team into the cottage, DCI Wallis knew that something terrible had occurred in this house. The smell of blood, urine, and rot was prominent. Fresh blood pooled on the aged living room carpet, and a wooden kitchen chair lay on its side. The frayed pieces of blue rope twine still attached to the arms told a sinister story. Following the blood droplets led horrifyingly to a scene of devastation in the cellar. The walls splashed with red blood and pink flesh like a disturbed Jackson Pollock painting. The bodies of two men lay on the floor. Lizzie Holland stood with her trembling hands on her head, staring at the wall. Skin as white as death with bare feet and sunken eyes in shadowy sockets.

'Get an ambulance crew down here now, for God's sake,' ordered DCI Wallis.

16

LIZZIE SCREAMED AT DAVID, and he could tell that she didn't immediately recognise him. His whole body had begun to shake, and he felt weak and sick. On unsteady legs, he made his way down the cellar stairs and knelt in front of Lizzie. At once, she was overcome with shock and emotion, falling forward into his arms like a helpless child. Not wanting to ask what she had been through, David proceeded to cut through the bonds that fastened her wrists and ankles together. Anger flashed through him as he saw the deep fissures in her skin. Lizzie's concern was immediately for him as her tender hand reached for his injured head. Her long-tangled hair fell away, revealing a painful-looking red line and purple bruising around her neck. Guilt and fury rose in David's chest. He didn't care what happened to himself; his priority was to get Lizzie out of this hell hole. The police would be here soon, and they would find the body.

As he helped Lizzie to her feet, his vision became blurry. Distant voices seemed to be telling him to do something, and it reminded him of being in the army. The last thing David remembered was Lizzie's pretty eyes before everything went black.

17

AMBER PHONED DAVID'S NUMBER FOR the third time. No answer, and Lizzie's mobile was still going straight to voicemail. Shouting up the stairs to her parents, Amber tried to reassure them.

'Mum I've just spoken to David. Everything is fine, don't worry', she lied. 'I'll be back to see you in the morning to explain'.

Margaret and George Evans were almost seventy years old, and Amber didn't want to risk making them ill with worry unless she had to. Driving the short distance to Lizzie and David's house, she pulled up on the empty driveway. Both cars were gone, but Amber knocked on the door anyway. This was crazy. It was almost one-thirty in the morning. What was going on?

Remembering her last conversation with David, Amber followed the directions to Rowan Cottage in a desperate attempt to get some answers. Flashing blue lights illuminated the dark country lane, and a police officer motioned for her to stop the car.

'Can I ask why you are driving this way, Miss?' asked the solemn-looking young officer.

Amber explained, and afterwards, she thought she detected a hint of pity in the eyes of the officer.

'You had better come with me, Miss Evans'.

Dread lay heavily in the pit of Amber's stomach as she was led past police cars, ambulances, and then two cars which she recognised. Two body bags were wheeled out of the cottage by the ambulance crew, and at that awful moment, Amber lost the contents of her stomach.

'Lizzie, oh God Lizzie. I'm so sorry, please no'. She cried in anguish. Looking up, she saw a third person being brought out of the open cottage door. This time they were alive. An official-looking woman with short blonde hair, wearing a grey suit, approached the young officer, and Amber could tell that they were talking about her. The woman in the suit walked over.

'Miss Evans, my name is Detective Chief Inspector Wallis, I understand you are the sister of Mrs Elizabeth Holland?'

'Lizzie, yes that's right. She's my sister; please can you tell me what's happening?'

The DCI walked Amber over to the ambulance.

'Lizzie is inside. She was held captive in that cottage, and although we don't have all the details yet, we believe your sister has been subjected to a violent assault. I'm sorry to have to inform you that your brother-in-law David has been fatally injured'.

18

LIZZIE KNEW THE MOMENT that David collapsed beside her that he was dead. She saw the light leave his eyes and instantly felt her heart stop. In a state of numbness, Lizzie was vaguely aware of a commotion. People were shouting, fussing, and lifting her onto something. It was all a blur. Life no longer had any meaning now that David was dead. Her loving husband and best friend was gone. He had saved her life and lost his own. Salty tears began to fall as she remembered David's handsome smile. His hearty laugh and his silly sense of humour. How his hands were always warm. How he would shower her in kisses and tell her that 'he loved her more'. Lizzie wished that she had died too. She didn't want to go on in a world without David. He had been her everything, and they had been really happy.

This entire nightmare was all her fault; why had she left her perfectly safe job in the pharmacy to follow a stupid dream? David would still be alive if only she had listened to everyone.

'Why? Why didn't I listen?' Lizzie asked herself in despair.

19

THE CLINICAL WHITE OF the hospital seemed impersonal and cold. DCI Cathy Wallis' functional black shoes silently walked down the corridor and entered the room. Lizzie Holland was sitting up in a crisply made bed, staring blankly out of the window. The abundance of flowers and cards did nothing to brighten the solemn atmosphere. A tray with some uneaten sandwiches sat on the side table next to a standard blue hospital chair.

Cathy sat down and gingerly touched Lizzie on the arm to get her attention. Lizzie had already given a statement, and it had been decided that Roy Peters' death was carried out in self-defence and that he had killed David Holland. DCI Wallis was here today to inform Lizzie of the motive that drove Roy to target her and David.

After seizing his computer and digging into his online history, the police discovered that Roy and David had been involved in a long-running and heated argument about fox hunting. David had been a passionate animal lover, and the debate had turned increasingly nasty. After an insult where David had called Roy a 'pathetic little fuckwit', the argument appeared to have abruptly ended. However, Roy had taken that insult to heart as it brought back painful childhood memories of when he had been continuously bullied. He used the power of social media to find out everything possible on David Holland. His life had been easy to piece together from all the snippets of information posted online.

After seeing the profile of David's darling little wife, Roy plotted his revenge. The fact that Lizzie had a mobile business seemed almost too good to be true. Using the dark web, he was able to buy Rohypnol, known as the 'date rape drug'.

Setting up the fake Facebook profile of seventeen-year- old Leanne Parker, he went on to make an appointment for Lizzie to come to his house. The plan had been to hold Lizzie captive and torture her until David figured out where she was. Once he had both Lizzie and David in his control, Roy had planned various methods of pain for each of them in turn, forcing the other to watch. He would Lord it over David, making sure he understood exactly who Roy was and why he was doing this. Eventually, after making David beg for forgiveness, Roy would shoot Lizzie in the head.

David would suffer terribly, watching helplessly as the love of his life had her brains blown out. Roy had intended to taunt David, telling him how this was all his fault, before finally killing him too. No one will ever know if, or how, Roy had planned to get away with it.

20

AMBER EVANS HAD HER sister all to herself again. It had been what she wanted but not like this. Lizzie had been inconsolable for a very long time after what

happened to her and David. She attempted suicide more than once and spent many months in therapy.

It was difficult to know what to do or say to help her little sister. This unimaginable, terrible thing had happened to her, and nothing could make it better.

Rowan Cottage had been boarded up and would become the infamous horror house of legend and ghost stories for future generations. Amber fought to have it demolished; she wanted to wipe out any trace of that madman who had caused her family so much pain, but she had lost the campaign. She couldn't imagine anyone would want to buy and renovate the place to live in, not after they learned of it's tragic history.

21

Eighteen months later.

LIZZIE HOLLAND STOOD IN front of the mirror. Her body was leaner now; her face was hardened. Cold, dead eyes that once were pretty stared back at the young widow. No longer weak and vulnerable, Lizzie had used her anger and grief to toughen up. Defined and strong muscles gave her an athletic appearance, and her mind was focused and disciplined. The scars on her neck and wrists had faded, hidden now by the shirt and long sleeves of her work uniform.

As she walked confidently through the station door, Lizzie felt a sense of purpose and she ignored the whispers behind her back. Everyone knew what had happened to her in that Godforsaken cottage. That's why she was here. Lizzie wanted to stop all the other

Roy Peters that might be out there, scuttling and stalking in the darkness. Hurting innocent people and taking their hearts away. Joining the police force at her age had been a brave decision for Lizzie. Her steely determination would see her advance up through the ranks, eventually making detective. Once she had the power, DI Lizzie Holland would stop at nothing to bring every single one of those fuckwits down.

The Depths Of Murder

1

FRANTICALLY SPRINTING THROUGH THE red-bricked alleys, DI Lizzie Holland raced to catch up with the hoody-clad fugitive. He was beginning to tire now and clumsily, he tripped, almost falling into the trio of wheelie bins that were blocking the narrow passage, slowing his pace. Seeing her opportunity, Lizzie hurled herself forward and rugby-tackled the hefty lad to the floor, where they both landed hard against the stone cobbles.

"Get off me, you crazy bitch!" shouted the struggling suspect as he tried to shake himself free.

"This is DI Holland, suspect apprehended behind Emmanuel Street, send backup, he's a feisty bugger, this one."

Sergeant Andrew Dove came bounding up the alley with a team of uniformed officers behind him.

The suspect was cuffed and read his rights before being marched off to the waiting police van.

"Bloody hell, ma'am, why didn't you wait for us? You could've been killed. You're the DI; you're meant to leave the donkey work to us lesser mortals."

"It's not my fault you young'uns can't keep up," Lizzie joked as she caught her breath and brushed the gravel from her trousers. "Anyway, you know how I am; can't risk the suspect getting away, had to bring him down when I had the chance."

The sergeant was beginning to learn that once his boss got her teeth into a case, Lizzie was like a lioness on the hunt and wouldn't let anything come between her and her prey.

Lizzie Holland was a rather unconventional DI, having only joined the Lancashire constabulary in her early forties after a personal tragedy changed her life forever. Nine years earlier, Lizzie had been kidnapped and tortured by a sadistic loner called Roy Peters. Peters also murdered her beloved husband David, who heroically rescued Lizzie. From that day on, Lizzie was hell-bent on joining the force to help prevent any other evil bastard from destroying other innocent lives.

The once timid and chubby Lizzie had transformed into a lean, mean, avenging angel who had joined the police on a fast-track training course and eventually worked her way up the ranks to Detective Inspector in the force's Major Investigation Team.

Lizzie was well-respected, and even though the other officers knew of her past tragedy, no one dared to show pity. Lizzie had apprehended many serious offenders in her short career and was a highly-driven DI. The members of Lizzie's team admired her courage and tenacity. The DCI, Maurice Piper, had been impressed by her from the start, recognising the signs of a great detective.

Back in her office, Lizzie coveted the cup of strong coffee that Verity brought over, a young constable who tended to be overeager at times. Thinking back on the afternoon's events, Lizzie knew that Dovey was right. She had been stupid to go chasing down a violent suspect like Danny Boyers on her own. Boyers had been arrested on suspicion of the rape and attempted murder of a lone female making her way home from the local pub, plus resisting arrest and threatening a police officer.

At almost fifty years old, Lizzie was no spring chicken, but after seeing the broken state of the victim with her face all smashed in, Lizzie wasn't going to let scum like Danny Boyers get away; not on her watch.

The following morning, after a steaming hot shower, Lizzie studied her naked reflection in the full-length mirror. Once, she would have avoided mirrors as her flabby stomach and chunky thighs upset her.

David used to love Lizzie's curvy body though and he always made her feel attractive. She wondered what he would think of her now. Lizzie's waist-length hair was now functionally short, and her body was lean and toned with the flat stomach she always dreamed of. Every evening after work, Lizzie liked to run the six miles home; the activity helped to clear her head, as well as keep her fit. One thing that hadn't changed though was her eyes; almond-shaped and deep hazel-brown, they were her best feature, and her mum used to say she had 'puppy dog eyes', which would often lead to Lizzie getting her way.

Pulling on the functional black work shoes and then packing her running trainers and shorts into the sports bag, a sudden movement at the kitchen window caught Lizzie's eye. It was a dark November morning and only six am, but something had triggered the security light.

Stepping outside, Lizzie could see nothing unusual. The plant pots on the small decking area were undisturbed, and the back gate was still bolted. Must have been a fox, she thought. Ensuring the door was locked, Lizzie turned to finish her coffee before heading to the train station. Walking down the garden path and onto the quiet street, Lizzie couldn't shake the feeling that she was being watched.

The call came while Lizzie was waiting for the train. The booming voice of her sergeant forced her to hold the phone away from her ear.

"Ma'am, we have a suspicious death at Stocks reservoir. It's a bad one so the sooner you get here the better."

"Okay Dovey, I'm still at Preston train station so pick me up from here and I'll see what's going on."

Lizzie was intrigued. Stocks reservoir was situated in the Trough of Bowland, a vast stretch of wilderness comprising dense woodland, rocky hills and wide-open moorland. Lizzie used to go there for picnics with her mum, dad and older sister when she was a kid. A beautiful place but very isolated in parts. It was years since she'd visited the area.

After informing her boss, DCI Maurice Piper, who will be the SIO in charge of the investigation, Lizzie walked to the front of the train station and impatiently waited. The DCI was nearing retirement and more than happy for Lizzie to head the team as deputy SIO, as long as she kept him updated. Lizzie felt proud that he had such trust in her capabilities; he knew she would get the job done.

Detective Sergeant Andrew Dove, or 'Dovey', as he was affectionately known, was leaning against the car talking loudly into his mobile phone. His thick, dark hair was styled in a bit of a quiff, as seemed to be the fashion for young men these days. Lizzie could hear that he was talking to an officer at the scene, instructing him to keep the public away from the area. Looking up, he saw Lizzie approach the car and ended the call.

"Morning boss," he said, half-yawning.

"Morning Dovey. Have I interrupted your lie-in?"

"Sorry," he said, yawning again. "The baby had a bad night and Keeley needed me to drive to the twenty-four-hour chemist for Calpol."

"Nothing serious?"

"Everything's fine, just a bit of teething. Mother and daughter were both sleeping like angels when I left this morning. Alright for some, eh?"

"Tell you what, we can grab a super-quick latte at the nearest Starbucks, and you can tell me all about this death."

For a few seconds, both Lizzie and Dovey sat in silence as the first sip of coffee was allowed to work its magic. Coffee was Lizzie's only addiction and probably one of the main reasons why she slept so poorly at night. The DS placed his cup in the holder and started the car.

"The body is that of a young female. Found floating on the surface of the reservoir by an early-morning fisherman. At first, he thought it was just a bag or something, but on looking closer through his binoculars, he saw long, blonde hair and phoned the police. Verity has taken his details and he's been allowed to go home. The old guy was pretty shaken up. James and the CSI team are already on their way so by the time we arrive, they should be all set up."

It was a thirty-mile drive from Preston train station to the large, secluded reservoir, which was a local beauty spot frequented by birdwatchers, fishermen and hikers. Driving up higher and higher towards the forest through the long country lanes, the sky was grey and overcast and made the surrounding moors even more imposing. The wilderness of the area brought back painful memories for Lizzie of the isolated cottage where she had been held captive all those years ago. The haunting beauty of the open countryside still held an ominous presence for her.

"I wouldn't fancy getting lost up here at this time of year," said Dovey, breaking Lizzie's thoughts.

"Me either. I used to come up here with my family as a kid you know, in the summer holidays. Me and Amber would paddle in the streams while Mum and Dad set up the folding picnic table."

"Sounds like you had a pretty good childhood, ma'am. I was lucky if my mum could tear herself away from the bingo long enough to make me beans on toast, and I've never met my dad."

Parked in the Stocks carpark in Gisburn Forest, Lizzie followed her sergeant through the Bowland countryside to the vast reservoir. The scene was a flurry of activity with CSIs. The police dive team had already retrieved the body. Careful not to disturb any possible evidence, they had covered her hands with sealed bags and bagged the body whilst still in the water, delicately manoeuvring her onto a stretcher and finally into the tent.

The trainee, Constable Verity Harris, approached Lizzie and DS Dovey with the excited demeanour of a child. This was her first major crime, and she was eager to prove herself.

"Hiya boss, the scene has been secured and we're keeping back any press. Apparently, there's a campsite not too far away – Slaidburn pitch-up – and I'm thinking there may be possible witnesses there."

"Campers? In the middle of November?" Dovey remarked, unable to understand why anyone would be mad enough to sleep outdoors at any time, never mind in winter.

"Hold your horses a minute, Verity. Was there any ID on the body?"

"Sorry ma'am, no, there was no ID found at all." Verity could've kicked herself for not thinking to mention it before rushing in.

Once gloved and booted in protective gear, Lizzie and DS Dovey were given access to the tent. Inside was the coroner, James Traynor, and the CSI team was busy with their investigations of the victim. Standing back, Lizzie made some observations of her own.

Although bloated, the deceased was clearly a young woman. Her hands had been fastened behind her back and grey duct tape wrapped around her eyes and mouth, leaving her nose uncovered. Bricks had been fastened to her ankles by brown, hessian-type rope. Whoever did this wanted to be sure the poor girl was never found. However, when the bodily gases were released, she began to float upwards, and the length of the rope was long enough for her body to be visible on the surface of the water.

Clothed in blue jeans and a black sweater with worn black and white canvas trainers, any visible skin was a horrid greenish black, with blisters and a waxy-looking shine. Long, blonde, matted hair lay sprawled out behind a once attractive face.

"Hello James. So what can you tell me so far?"

James Traynor was tall and thin, causing him to stoop to get out of the tent. His glasses peered out beneath the white hood and mask, making him look older than his forty-nine years.

"Considering the water temperature and the discolouration of the skin, gas formation and putridity, I'd estimate she has been in the water less than a week, although Sabine will be able to tell you more back at the lab. I'll be ordering a post-mortem and officially listing it as a homicide. You'll have my report before the end of the day."

"Okay, great. Are there any signs of the cause of death, besides the obvious, I mean? Can you tell if the victim was dead before she was dropped into the water? Any bruising or strangulation marks on the body?"

Lizzie wasn't hopeful for evidence with the body having been submerged in the water, and she was looking for anything that could give some clue as to what happened in this girl's final moments.

"Not on the first examination, no. There appear to be no obvious injuries that could have caused her death. Apart from a nasty bruise to her left temple, possibly from a fist, hard enough to render the victim unconscious but not so severe as to be the cause of death, unfortunately, it is likely she was still alive when she went into the water. Death by asphyxiation I would say, but the post-mortem will confirm that for definite."

"Thanks James, I'll follow up with Sabine then later."

Lizzie and Dovey stood looking out over the reservoir. The gloomy clouds were reflected in the glass-like water. Low surrounding hills seemed to be respectfully watching as the victim's body was transferred into the waiting van.

"If only those hills could talk," Dovey said in a melancholy tone.

"No point in wishing for the impossible, Dovey. We've got a real job to find whoever did this. The Trough of Bowland is a massive area and so remote. But we've got to get them, Dovey, we have to bring them to justice. Whoever that girl was, she didn't deserve to die. She would have suffered, Andy."

"Don't worry, ma'am, we'll get them. We'll get them if it's the last thing we ever do."

As the rope, bricks and all other evidence were bagged and tagged, Lizzie made a note for her team to follow up with the pathologist.

"Right, hopefully, Sabine will be able to retrieve some DNA but, in the meantime, get Verity on to Missing Persons with the description of our dead girl. Someone must be missing her. Then both of you go to that campsite just in case someone is daft enough to be staying there. If there's a reception area or website, get details of anyone who was there in the past week, and statements of anything they might've seen or heard. After that, you can follow up with the elderly man that reported the body. But Dovey, leave me the car keys."

Back at the lab, Sabine Monera, the pathologist, was conducting the post-mortem. Having moved to the UK from Italy as a child, Sabine had flourished in school and decided to follow in her father's footsteps. Although he was himself retired, Sabine often visited Bernard for advice and intellectual discussions over lemon tea. Since her mother passed away, their relationship had grown stronger than ever.

"Hello, my dear. I am so sorry that this has happened to you. Don't you worry though, there is no one better at finding the monster who killed you. Lizzie Holland will get you justice. Now, I will do my part in helping her but I'm afraid I must make some intrusions, but I know you understand why."

Sabine always liked to talk to the victims. She treated them like people, who were once animated and had a voice. A laugh, a special smile maybe. Individualities that meant something. After performing the preliminary examinations of the body, respectfully and carefully, Sabine made the first cut.

Driving back to Hutton police station, Lizzie mulled the case over. Their priority was to identify the victim and inform any family of her death before social media or the local news leaked it. Someone had to have driven the victim up here intending to kill her. The ropes, the cement bricks; this was premeditated. Whatever the reason, they wanted the victim to experience fear and suffering. Lizzie could feel anger and the need for vengeance rising inside her.

"Watch out, you cruel piece of shit, I'm coming for you," Lizzie spoke out loud, and it made her feel empowered.

DS Andrew Dovey approached the campsite with relief. Verity had not shut up talking for the full ten-minute drive, except when they stopped to interview any passing hikers. He knew she was excited about her first murder investigation and eager to impress, but the lack of sleep was catching up with him now and his patience was wearing thin.

2

AFTER MUCH BICKERING, TERRY and Emma Forshaw had finally managed to erect the two-man tent.

"Remind me again, Terry, why we decided to rough it instead of booking a nice, comfortable hotel?" Emma asked her newly-wedded husband.

"I thought you liked nature and the countryside. You wanted to do yoga under the stars, you said. Anyway, hotels cost a fortune." Terry unfolded his camping chair and took a can of Fosters from the cool box.

"It didn't take you long to start on the booze, Terry. Isn't it a bit early, even for you?" He looked like a right idiot, she thought, sitting there in his scarf and gloves, trying to open a cold can.

"For God's sake, woman, stop your mithering. I'm on holiday. Aren't I allowed a drink on my holiday?" Terry hated Emma's constant nagging about his drinking; so, he liked a couple of beers after a hard day's work. It wasn't as though he was an alcoholic.

Emma sighed and began to unpack the camping stove and kettle.

Slaidburn pitch-up was a pop-up campsite in a remote part of Gisburn Forest. Surrounded by trees and roughly a mile from the edge of Stocks reservoir, known as a place of peace and seclusion for those wanting to get away from the noise and bustle of towns and cities. Terry was recommended the campsite by his friend. Usually, they would prefer to stay in a hotel or B&B, but despite only being married six months, she and Terry had been arguing a lot lately and he thought a change might do them good.

Just as the kettle had boiled, Emma heard voices behind them and turned to see a smartly-dressed man and woman approaching the site.

The campsite was empty except for the one small tent pitched in a small clearing. It had been difficult to find as apparently, it was just a wild camping place, free of charge, and no need to pre-book. The area was a registered dark sky area so was great for star-gazing in the winter months.

"Sorry to disturb you both. I'm DS Andrew Dove and this is Constable Harris. We're with the Lancashire Police and are investigating a murder over at Stocks reservoir."

"Jesus Christ!" Terry almost fell off his chair as he jumped up, but somehow managed not to spill his beer. "A murder?"

"I'm afraid so, sir. The body of a young female was found floating in the water early this morning. We'd like to ask you both a few questions."

"Us? We didn't see anything, did we, Terry?" Emma was nervous and suddenly, this tranquil woodland seemed haunting and dangerous.

"No, not a thing. We were the only ones on the road on the way in here."

"What time did you arrive in the area today and what made you decide to camp all the way out here in the middle of winter?" the DS asked the shocked couple, as Verity stood poised with notepad and pen.

"Well, we set off from home about eight o clock and we got here at nine-thirty, I reckon. We only live in Leyland, so it isn't that far really. Emma wanted to see the stars without all the usual light pollution so that's why we're here."

Verity decided to take the initiative before the DS could ask his next question. "How did you find this place? I mean, it's pretty out of the way."

Emma turned her attention to the young officer, neat as a pin in her navy suit and black boots. She could tell she was a proud and eager policewoman who didn't want to be left out of the conversation. Good for her, Emma thought.

"Terry's friend owns the café over at the Gisburn fly-fishery. He was the one who said we should come here."

"The fly-fishery? Is that nearby, and what is the full name of the café owner please?" Verity was scribbling away, enjoying the feel of real police work.

Terry flashed his wife a dark look before answering. "The fishery is on the other side of the water, on the bank of the reservoir. The owner of the café is called Jenson Thomas."

"We'll have to speak to Mr Thomas and any other staff at the fishery and the café. Does Mr Thomas own the fishery too?" Dovey got his question in quick before Verity could rush in again.

"Yeah, he jointly owns the café and fishery with his dad, Clive, and his girlfriend, Roxie, helps out."

"That's great, thanks. Is that your van parked over there?" pointing to the blue transit van.

"Yeah, that's mine. I'm a builder by trade. It came in handy to fit all the camping gear in."

"And did you stop anywhere on the way here at all?" Dovey was thinking they may have seen someone leaving the crime scene.

Emma was just about to speak when Terry quickly interrupted her. “Straight here from Leyland. Emma was keen to get everything set up, then we could relax and enjoy the day, isn’t that right, love?”

“Yeah, that’s right. I wanted to make sure we found a good spot and got sorted before it started to go dark.”

“Okay. If you don’t mind, I’d like to have a look around while Constable Harris takes your details, just in case we need to speak to you again.”

Dovey walked over to the van and took down the registration number for an ANPR check later. The van was very clean apart from the fresh mud and leaves from the drive into the woods; too clean, he thought, for a builder’s work van. Peering inside, he could see a bottle of orange juice and a can of Pepsi in the front, plus a few charger cables and a dash-cam.

“You mind if I look in the back of the van, sir?” the DS shouted over to the man.

He was dressed in a blue, woollen beanie hat and matching gloves, a grey scarf and a Nike tracksuit. Mid-thirties, Dovey thought, although his skin was rough and tanned, perhaps making him appear older than he was. The wife, Emma, was petite and blonde, younger, with a nervous disposition. He was sure she had wanted to say something earlier, but her husband had butted in before she had the chance.

"Sure, go ahead. It's not locked."

Pulling the doors open, Dovey could see nothing untoward in the back of the van. A pair of wellies, some cartons of milk and gas canisters for the camping stove. Again, the van was exceptionally clean. He picked up the wellies and looked at the soles. They looked quite new and a size 5 so probably belonged to the wife.

"Did you have the dash-cam on when you drove here?" Dovey's mind was sharp again now and ideas were running around in his mind.

"Nah, I never bother with it. It's only there because Emma insisted after I had a little bump a while ago."

The disappointment in the DS was palpable as he walked back to the tent.

"Got everything you need, Constable?"

"Yes, sarge. Mr and Mrs Forshaw have given me their full details and have agreed to get in touch if they think of anything that could be relevant."

"Right, thank you both for your time. One last question, Mr Forshaw. How does a builder keep his van as clean as that?"

"Oh, I always get it valeted before we go on holiday. I don't like turning up to a new place with a scruffy-looking van."

"I see. Well, listen, I know you've only just got here but I suggest you pack up and go elsewhere. There's a dangerous killer who may still be in the area. I hear the Lake District is very nice."

With that, the DS and Verity made their way back to the car, wondering how they could tell Lizzie that they had no witnesses yet. Perhaps the old man who found the body had remembered something more.

After watching the police car drive away, Terry gave a long whistle and sigh of relief. Emma had been like a coiled spring the whole time though and finally let it all out.

"What the hell, Terry? Why did you lie to the police? You were here yesterday working and you only picked me up from the train station at nine this morning. What were you really doing, Terry?"

"Stop panicking, Emma. I just had a bit of business. Jenson's thinking of extending the café and wanted me to have a look, and give him a quote. I slept in the van last night and there was no need to tell the police; it had nothing to do with any murder. And you giving Jenson's name to them has probably just landed us all in hot water. I'd better phone and warn him."

3

BACK AT THE STATION, LIZZIE turned on the coffee machine and then phoned Dovey for an update. She was frustrated to hear that the campsite and surrounding area hadn't provided any witnesses to the murder, however, the fly-fishing place could yield new information. Dovey and Verity had been round there but it was closed, so Lizzie asked them to return to the station. She would visit the fishery herself in the morning. It had been a difficult day and there was still so much work to do. Lizzie was starving and placed an order online for a chippy tea for her and the team.

A head popped around Lizzie's door. It was the smiling face of Sally from the Missing Person Department.

"Hi, I've run the description of your murder victim through the database, and I think we have a match. Twenty-year-old Charity Fitzpatrick. She was reported missing Friday night by her mum. I've sent a copy to your e-mail."

"Thanks, Sally. Let's hope Sabine has some DNA for me, then we can formally confirm if it's her or not."

Lizzie quickly opened the file on the missing girl. A photo of a pretty, young woman stared back at her from the screen. Long, blonde hair like a Barbie doll and green eyes. It was hard to relate the bloated corpse at the reservoir to this beautiful girl who looked so full of life.

Another knock on Lizzie's door. This time, it was DS Dovey and DC Harris. The irresistible smell of freshly-cooked chips followed them into the room.

"Hiya boss. The Just Eat guy was outside with your order. I think you must be a mind-reader, ma'am; my stomach thinks my throat's been cut." Dovey couldn't get the chip wrappers open fast enough.

Verity warned Dovey about eating her chips before going to make a fresh coffee for everyone.

"Is that a chippy I can smell wafting into my office?"

The broad Preston accent of DCI Maurice Piper made them all jump. A tall but well-fed man in his late fifties with a surprisingly thick head of grey hair and a friendly smile. He walked over to Lizzie and stole a couple of chips from her tray.

"Careful, sir, they're still quite hot."

Lizzie had a good relationship with the DCI, and though he was winding down his responsibilities now, he was still a good detective with a wealth of experience. He had been an invaluable mentor to her, and she respected him greatly.

"I believe you've all had a tough day, so I'll let you off for not buying me any chips, but I expect an update from you in half an hour, Lizzie." Then, after pinching more chips this time from Dovey, the DCI strolled back to his office.

"What did Spud want? Are we in trouble 'cause of the chips?" Verity's whispering voice asked as she came back with the coffee.

"Don't let the DCI hear you calling him that, Verity, or he'll have you back on the front desk before you can finish that brew."

Lizzie knew all the officers called the DCI 'Spud' behind his back, and it was no wonder with a name like Maurice Piper.

The incident room was filled with the serious faces of the investigation team and also the DCI who was perched on the edge of a desk at the rear.

"Right, everyone, this is what we know so far." Lizzie addressed the room confidently and had a commanding presence as she relayed the information onto the large whiteboard next to her. "The body of a young female was found floating in Stocks reservoir just after six am this morning by a local fisherman. She had been murdered most horrifically, weighed down with bricks and thrown into the water while she was still alive. Dovey and Verity have followed up with the man who discovered the body and he's been ruled out of our inquiries due to the fact he has an alibi for the time of death. There's a fly-fishery, café and wild campsite nearby. There was only one couple on the campsite and they've been interviewed, and the fishery/café was closed. Dovey and I will pay another visit first thing tomorrow. Missing Persons came up with a positive match for our victim; Charity Fitzpatrick, aged twenty, has been missing from her home in Garstang after going to meet with a friend on Friday afternoon. Seen getting into a taxi at two pm by her mum, Lorna Fitzpatrick. The taxi driver has confirmed he dropped Charity off at Barton Grange Garden Centre just after two-ten that day. This is the last sighting of Charity alive that we know of.'

"According to the pathologists' report, the fingerprints had been sloughed off due to her time in the water, but Sabine has confirmed from dental records that our victim is indeed Charity Fitzpatrick. The family have been notified and a formal ID will be made by Charity's mum. There are no signs of injuries to the body, apart from where the ropes had chaffed the wrists and ankles, and a bruise to her head, perhaps how her attacker initially managed to grab Charity. There was no DNA so even though the bruise appears to be from someone's fist, they must have been wearing gloves. Due to the residue in the victim's nostrils, organ temperature and other contributing factors listed in the report, death by drowning/asphyxiation is the official cause of death and she estimated the time of the murder to be between seven pm and midnight Friday.

"So, Charity gets into a taxi at two pm yesterday and is murdered by midnight. We need to know who this friend was she was due to meet and what happened in those hours before Charity's death. How did she get to Stocks reservoir and why? Verity, get on to Barton Grange and ask to see their CCTV. This friend might be on camera if they turned up. And speak to the taxi firm again to see if the driver remembers anything else, anything Charity may have mentioned that didn't seem important at the time. Check the driver dropped Charity where he said he did. We can't rule anyone out as a suspect right now. DS Dove and I will go and speak to Charity's mum tonight and then we'll call it a day. First thing in the morning, I want you to find out who Charity hung out with, boyfriends, girlfriends, knock on doors and check her social media and bank records. Leave no stone unturned. Someone wanted this girl dead, and they went to enormously cruel lengths to do it; we must find them before they kill again."

Garstang is a pretty, little Lancashire village surrounded by farmer's fields and country pubs. The house that Charity had called home was a stunning barn conversion with floor-to-ceiling glass windows.

"How the other half live, eh, ma'am?" Dovey looked on enviously at the Mercedes on the long drive.

"I bet she'd give it all up in a heartbeat if it brought her daughter back, Andy." Lizzie had learned to be grateful for the simple life.

The door to the house was opened by the family liaison officer who had been providing support to Mrs Fitzpatrick.

"Hi, DI Lizzie Holland and DS Andrew Dove. We need to ask Mrs Fitzpatrick a few questions if she's feeling up to it."

"Hello, I'm Rebecca Foster, her appointed FLO. I'm afraid Mrs Fitzpatrick is still in shock, so I don't know how helpful she'll be. The ex-husband lives in the US with his new wife. He's been informed but he wasn't really in the picture anymore; it was just Lorna and Charity for years, so they had a very close relationship. Come through to the lounge."

Returning her warrant card to her pocket, Lizzie followed the FLO into the grand house. Furnished with designer curtains and solid oak furniture with delicate glass ornaments purposely placed here and there, it was like stepping into a show house. Polished wooden floorboards caused the footsteps of the three officers to echo up to the tall ceilings. There wasn't a trace of dust anywhere.

"I bet she doesn't buy her accessories from B&M bargains."

"Shut up, Dovey, and show some respect!" Lizzie whispered back. Her sergeant was a very capable partner, but he could be tactless at times.

Lorna Fitzpatrick was sat on the green, velvet sofa clutching a framed photograph of her and Charity in happier times. Tears had made her blue eyes red and swollen. When the detectives walked into the room, she looked up and pushed a strand of poker-straight hair behind her ear. Lorna Fitzpatrick bore a striking resemblance to her daughter.

"Lorna, this is DI Holland and DS Dovey. Are you up to answering a few questions?"

"We are so sorry for your loss, Mrs Fitzpatrick." Lizzie thought the woman had the look of a rag doll – limp and lifeless; all the hope and joy had been drained from her.

"Can you tell us about the last time that you saw your daughter?"

Taking a deep breath, the grieving mother described how her daughter had been texting a friend and they had arranged to meet.

"We didn't find any of Charity's belongings at the scene. Can you describe any bag she may have taken with her? And also, do you know the name of the friend as we'll need to speak with them too?"

"Charity always used her favourite brown backpack. It was Louis Vuitton and had the standard brown, two-tone pattern. As for the friend, I don't know who it was. Charity just said it was an old friend who had recently gotten back in touch. They intended on having a glass of wine or two so Charity had booked a taxi. I'd been glad to see her getting on with life again after what she'd been through."

Lizzie shot Dovey a questioning look. "What had she been through, Mrs Fitzpatrick?"

"I thought you would already know. In the summer, Charity had been sexually assaulted when she was waitressing at Gisburn café. She reported it to the police and the trial date was set for this Tuesday. There's no way she would have missed it. Charity was strong and didn't want him getting away with what he had done to her."

Dovey could see Lizzie's whole demeanour change; a fire had been lit in her.

"Who was the man, Mrs Fitzpatrick? Who did Charity say assaulted her?"

"It was the owner of the café, Jenson Thomas."

4

DOVEY DROPPED LIZZIE AT HOME just after nine pm that evening. Her mind was whirling at what Mrs Fitzpatrick had told her about the assault on Charity. Phone calls had been made immediately and her team had sent her the details.

Charity had been working at the fly-fishery café when one evening, her friend Roxie, the owner's girlfriend, went home unwell, leaving her to lock up alone. After closing time, Charity had been cleaning when Jenson Thomas turned up to take cash from the safe. It was then that Jenson forced Charity into the back room and held one hand against her throat while his other was up her skirt. Charity had been moments away from being raped when Roxie had turned up to say she was feeling better but had left her mobile phone in the café earlier. Jenson had warned Charity that if she told anyone what he'd done, he would kill her; that he knew people who could hurt her.

When interviewed, Jenson had denied the whole thing and said Charity had been jealous of his relationship with Roxie and had made the whole thing up after he refused her advances. Roxie defended him and said Charity was never a friend, just the local bored rich girl who was used to getting her own way. However, Charity had been clever and had saved the underwear, which showed Jenson's DNA and also, swabs from Charity proved he'd had sexual contact with her. Knowing he was likely to be convicted once it went to court, Jenson changed his story, saying it was consensual. His father bailed him out of custody and the trial date had been set. Jenson had no previous convictions but after speaking to the locals, he was known for lending money at sky-high interest rates with nefarious 'friends' who would collect any overdue payments and hand out violent beatings to those who couldn't pay.

Lizzie couldn't wait to interview him, but for now, she needed to sleep. Pouring herself a large glass of toffee vodka and swallowing a sleeping tablet, she fell onto the bed in her fluffy pyjamas. The bedroom curtains were open and Orion's Belt shone brightly in the clear winter sky. As Lizzie gazed out at the stars, eyes beginning to get heavy, a sudden noise that sounded like the letterbox swam into her head. The vodka and the Zopiclone had taken effect though and Lizzie was out for the count.

The next morning, Lizzie's alarm woke her at five-thirty, but raring to go, she grabbed her car keys and headed for the front door. There'd be no jogging home until this case was over. On the jute mat behind the door lay a white envelope. No stamp or address so it had been hand-delivered. Curiously, she carefully opened the sealed envelope and removed a piece of paper that had one name typed in capital letters: ROY PETERS.

Lizzie dropped the paper in shock, and memories of a weasel-faced man forcing a plastic bag over her head until she almost lost consciousness over and over again flashed into her mind. What kind of a sick joke was this? Roy Peters was dead; she was there when David blew his brains out all those years ago. Lizzie didn't have time for this. She made a mental note to check her CCTV when she got home. She put the envelope and letter in an evidence bag and would take it to the lab for testing later. Right now, she had to focus on the murder investigation at hand, and Jenson Thomas was going to get both barrels if he dared to bullshit Lizzie today.

Gisburn café was just opening when Lizzie and Dovey arrived. A girl in her twenties with strikingly bright, cherry-red, spiked hair was just putting out the advertising board. She wore a name badge, so they knew this was Roxie, Jenson Thomas's girlfriend.

"Can we have a word?" Dovey approached the girl holding up his ID card, along with Lizzie.

"If this is about that murder, I don't know anything. I was at home with my fella all Friday night. We didn't hear or see anything before you ask."

"How did you know about the murder, Roxie…?"

"Clarke. My name's Roxanne Clarke. A mate of Jenson's was interviewed by you, and he phoned to let us know. I've had dealings with your lot before. I was questioned a few months back about some so-called assault on an employee here. She claimed my Jenson tried to rape her. Stuck-up little bitch."

Well, Roxanne, that 'stuck-up little bitch' was found murdered yesterday morning in the reservoir barely a mile from here. Perhaps Jenson wanted her silenced for good before she could testify in court?" Lizzie almost spat the words out, her fury threatening to get the better of her.

Roxanne didn't appear to be shocked or upset by the news that the murder victim was her former colleague and friend.

"Well, if someone decided to kill precious, little Charity, it's got nothing to do with us. She probably accused someone else of rape and they wouldn't stand for it."

"But Jenson admitted to having sexual relations with Charity. Doesn't that bother you that he cheated on you?" Dovey was trying to incite a reaction from her.

"That was all Charity's doing, leading him on. He made a mistake, and he said it was a one-off. He was sorry and he loves me, so I decided to forgive him. None of us is perfect and anyway, he bought me this soon after."

Roxie waved her left hand to show a huge diamond engagement ring glittering in the winter sun.

"So, he bought you off then?" Lizzie couldn't help herself and Dovey raised his eyebrows at her audacity.

"No one bought anyone off. I love Roxie and I want to marry her. What happened with Charity is in the past." Jenson Thomas was tall and muscular with fair hair, an attractive man in his early thirties. Lizzie could see how some women might be charmed by him.

"You must be Mr Thomas. We're investigating the murder of Charity Fitzpatrick whose body was discovered early yesterday morning floating in the reservoir. But I guess you already knew this?"

"I knew there'd been a murder as my mate Terry was camping nearby, but I didn't know it was Charity, I swear."

Lying bastard, Lizzie thought to herself.

"When was the last time either of you saw Charity?"

"Not since the accusation. Obviously, she didn't return to work, and neither of us wanted anything to do with her."

"And where were you both on Friday between seven pm and midnight?"

"Me and my dad closed up the café and fishery at five pm and I dropped Dad at his and carried on straight home. Roxie has Fridays off so Dad helps out. We watched a bit of telly then had an early night. On Saturday morning, me and Roxie got up for work but Terry called and said someone had been killed so we kept the cafe closed out of respect, plus Terry said the whole area was cordoned off."

"And Roxie, where were you on Friday then?"

"Nowhere, I stayed at home all day to do the housework and have tea ready for my Jenson when he got home."

Lizzie pictured Roxie in her vintage apron playing house.

"Does the café and fishery have CCTV?" Lizzie was looking inside the café now, but she couldn't see any cameras.

"Nah, no need for it here. We don't see much crime in this neck of the woods, usually."

"Are there any other employees besides the two of you?"

"No, just us since Charity left. My dad is the joint owner but he's a sleeping partner and just comes in on Fridays. He's in his seventies."

"And what about your other business, Mr Thomas? We believe you might be a bit of a loan shark on the side. That you have violent associates who hand out beatings to those who can't pay you back on time." Dovey could tell the question had rattled him.

"That's a lie. The fishery and café are doing well so I like to help out people in the community who are short on cash. I charge a fair rate and they know I expect to be paid back on time. It's a legitimate business, all above board."

"We hear different, that people are scared of you and your heavies. That you prey on the desperate and then threaten to hurt them if they don't pay up. Just like you threatened to kill Charity if she told anyone about the sexual assault." Lizzie was on a roll now.

"Listen, I've been through all that already. Charity consented!"

"Yet we only have your word to that now, don't we, Mr Thomas, seeing as someone took Charity, weighed her down with bricks and threw her in the middle of the reservoir!"

Lizzie's blood was boiling, and she had to walk out of the café to calm down.

"I've taken their details and said we'll be in touch if we need to speak to them again. Are you alright, ma'am?"

"They're both lying through their teeth, Dovey. I know he had something to do with Charity's death. It's too much of a coincidence that she was murdered right before testifying against him. I want warrants for their phone records, background checks, and see if you can find any CCTV on the roads leading from their home address to here on the day and night of the murder, and the same for that couple on the campsite. There's a connection between them all and I don't like it one bit."

That evening, Lizzie stayed late at the station, de-briefing the rest of the team and updating the DCI on the investigation. Before she left for home, Lizzie dropped the envelope she'd received into the lab for testing. This case was pushing all of her buttons and she didn't like how it was making her feel. Lizzie knew she'd lost her temper at the café earlier and was disappointed in herself. What she needed was a hot bath to soak away her tension.

Dropping the lavender-scented bath bomb into the water, Lizzie stepped in and lay back, letting the heat melt away all her swirling thoughts.

"Alexa, play The Lark Ascending." The Vaughan Williams piece was a favourite of Lizzie's and it always helped to calm her.

Before going to bed, Lizzie remembered about checking her CCTV. Watching the footage from the previous night, she was horrified to see that at one-fourteen am, the silent figure of a man dressed in black posted the envelope through her door. His face was covered in a balaclava, so it was difficult to see any identifying features. Rewinding the footage further back to the morning of the murder, when the security light had been triggered, Lizzie saw the back of what seemed to be the same man disappearing over the back gate. Lizzie sat back in shock. This can't be happening, not here in her own home.

It was late in the evening, but Lizzie phoned Dovey and told him about the CCTV and the letter. He had wanted to come straight round but Lizzie wouldn't let him; she just needed someone to talk it over with.

"Sorry for disturbing you, Andy. I hope I didn't wake the little one. I'm fine, it was just a shock, but I feel better now I've got it off my chest."

Dovey reassured her and insisted on sending a uniformed officer round to watch over Lizzie's house, but once again, she refused. Lizzie didn't want the force to think she was weak and afraid. After what happened to her before, Lizzie vowed that she would never be a victim again.

Double-checking the locks, Lizzie went to bed clutching David's old fishing knife under her pillow.

5

AFTER A FITFUL NIGHT'S SLEEP, Lizzie woke feeling restless and agitated. Eager to get to the station, she downed her coffee and headed out the door. Addressing her team that morning, she wanted updates and hoped for a solid lead.

"Good morning, everyone. I appreciate you all coming in on a Sunday, and overtime has been given the okay by the boss." On hearing this, the team let out a cheer and the DCI gave a nod at the back of the room.

"So, let's get up to speed." Lizzie gained the attention of everyone once more. "Verity, any luck with the CCTV from the garden centre?"

"Yes, boss. Barton Grange Garden Centre shows Charity getting out of the taxi at two-ten pm, just like the driver said. The taxi firm confirmed he returned to the rank at two-thirty pm and didn't leave for his next fare until three pm. The CCTV also shows Charity waiting at the garden centre for a few minutes before being approached by this person. They headed inside and left two hours later. Both are then picked up on camera leaving the carpark on foot, and that's when we lose sight of them."

DC Verity Harris was excited to show Lizzie the footage.

As Lizzie viewed the CCTV image, the friend Charity had arranged to meet walked into the frame; the cherry-red hair of Roxanne Clarke was unmistakable.

"Dovey, get yourself down to Gisburn café now. Take a couple of uniform with you and bring in Roxanne Clarke. She lied to us and I want to know why."

Whilst DS Dove rushed out of the office, the rest of the team gave what other information they had.

Sat in the DCI's office, Lizzie discussed the investigation with her superior.

"So, sir, the couple we interviewed from the campsite are also lying, as multiple traffic cameras picked up Terry Forshaw's van driving up the M6 Friday afternoon, not Saturday morning as they told us. Also, Terry is clearly alone in the van, meaning he didn't arrive with his wife. Verity and uniform have gone to bring them both in for further questioning but I need to stay here to interview Roxanne Clarke. Jenson Thomas's father, Clive, confirmed his alibi for Friday up until dropping him at home about five-thirty pm. Unfortunately, though, due to the remote location, there are no traffic cameras on the country roads that lead to Jenson and Roxanne's address. They live in the middle of nowhere. My gut feeling is that they're hiding something. Charity's bag and mobile phone are still missing. The bag was an expensive one so if it has been dumped, it may be that someone has found it and decided to keep it. I think it's time to hold a press conference, sir."

DCI Piper listened intently without interrupting his DI.

"Lizzie, I have faith in your instincts but media coverage now might cause chaos. Are you certain the entire scene has been searched thoroughly?"

"Yes sir, the Dive Team in the water and the Dog Search Team have been over the entire area. I really think informing the public now might give us more leads and possible witnesses."

Lizzie was feeling on edge.

"Okay, Lizzie, you can arrange a press conference if the mother agrees to it, but Lizzie, keep your head and your temper. I know this case has hit a bit close to home but I need you to stay focused, is that understood?"

"Yes, sir, loud and clear."

Lizzie wondered if Dovey had dobbed her in about getting angry at the café.

Roxanne Clarke sat opposite Lizzie and Dovey in the brightly-lit interview room. She looked worried but defiant too and refused a solicitor. The heating was on full whack, making the room feel hot and sickly. Lizzie thought Roxanne must be sweating in her rainbow woollen scarf and big overcoat. Once the recorder was running, Lizzie identified everyone present and began the interview.

"Tell me why you lied to us, Roxanne. You met up with Charity on Friday afternoon and left together. Where did you go after the garden centre?"

Roxanne took a sip of her water; her painted pink fingernails were a stark contrast to the white plastic cup.

"I'm not lying, I didn't meet up with her. I told you, I was at home all day on Friday."

Dovey spun the computer screen around to face Roxie.

"This is CCTV footage from the garden centre on Friday. There is Charity waiting and then… oh, look, that's you isn't it, Roxie? You're wearing the same rainbow scarf as today. So, I think it's about time you started telling us the truth; otherwise, you could be facing a murder charge."

As Roxie watched the footage, her features changed and she broke down in tears.

"Okay, okay. I lied." She sniffed. "I didn't want Jenson to find out. The day that Charity was assaulted in the café, I saw more than I let on. I saw Jenson pin Charity against the wall. I heard him threaten to kill her."

"So, why did you blame Charity if you knew the truth?" Lizzie was incredulous.

"Because I'm of terrified of him. Jenson has a temper and he will never let me leave. He says that I belong to him. I messaged Charity in secret and told her that I believed her and that I wanted to meet to discuss the trial. The only way I could ever escape Jenson is if he went to prison. Charity was a nice girl and said she understood. We met up over a glass of wine or two and I was going to speak to a solicitor about my testifying in court. Only, Saturday morning when I heard about the murder, I knew; I knew in my heart it was Charity and that Jenson had killed her, just like he said he would. All my hopes of escape were shattered."

"That still doesn't explain where you and Charity went after leaving the garden centre."

Roxanne finally removed her scarf and wiped her eyes with it, causing black mascara to smudge across her cheek. The uniformed officer who had been standing in the corner handed her a tissue.

"Thanks. The thing is, Jenson will kill me if he finds this out. I've been having an affair with one of the lads that works for him. Terry Forshaw. He's married but we've been meeting up in the woods for a month now. I met him when he came to measure up for a new countertop at the café."

"Ma'am, Terry Forshaw is the guy we questioned at the campsite along with his wife, Emma. Is this the man you mean, Roxanne?" Dovey showed her a profile picture of Terry.

"Yeah, that's him. He's a builder and the job he was doing at the café was a perfect excuse for being up here so often. His wife didn't suspect a thing. Terry said they should never have got married in the first place; they were too different."

Lizzie disapproved. She always believed if you weren't happy then it's kinder to end the relationship rather than lie and cheat.

"So, what does Terry have to do with Charity?"

"I phoned him to pick me and her up from the garden centre, but Charity said she would get a taxi home. Terry picked me up in his van and we went to our usual place for a bit in the woods. I never saw Charity again." Roxie began to cry once more. "There's something else. When I got home at five pm after being with Terry, I expected Jenson about six-thirty, but he didn't come home until long after midnight. When we heard about the murder, he forced me to lie for him."

"So, you don't have anyone to corroborate your own alibi either, Roxanne?"

The girl was suddenly startled.

"I guess not. But I've told you everything now, I promise."

Back in the main office, as Lizzie and Dovey sat waiting for the coffee machine to brew, they discussed the interview.

"Do you believe her, boss? Is that why you released her? I think I do. Those tears were real and she seems genuinely afraid of Jenson."

"I don't know, Andy. I've no real evidence to charge her though and she knows not to leave the area. I'll feel better when we've got Terry Forshaw's version of events. At least now we know why he was driving up here on Friday alone; it was for his rendezvous with Roxie. But it still doesn't explain why he lied about it."

"Perhaps, ma'am, he was trying to protect Roxie and himself. He didn't want to risk it getting back to Jenson or Emma?"

"That's plausible, yeah. Verity will have to conduct the interview though. As soon as we get the search warrant, you and I will hotfoot it down to Jenson's home address, and I'll send a team to search the café and fishery. If we find one tiny scrap of evidence that he had something to do with Charity's death, I'll have him, Andy; I'll make sure he never sees the light of day again."

Just as Lizzie was about to take a bite of her sandwich, she received a call from Verity.

"Ma'am, we have a problem. Terry Forshaw has been found beaten to death."

6

LIZZIE AND THE TEAM HAD worked late into the night. With a second murder and still no arrests, the investigation was beginning to take its toll. Tempers were frayed at the briefing due to frustration and over-tiredness. Despite there still being so much work to do, Lizzie sent everyone home; she may not have a family but others did and she had to keep that in mind.

Unable to rest, Lizzie stayed at the station. Even though Dovey had a young child, he also insisted on staying.

"I'll get more peace and quiet here than I will at home, boss. Keeley has got her mother over to help out with the baby, and anyway, I want to keep working on the investigation."

Keen to prove her dedication, Verity had also volunteered to work through the night. Lizzie was glad of the company and hoped that between them, they could make some progress.

"Thanks for staying, you two. I'll see the big man pays you the extra. I think we need to go back to the beginning of this case. Let's go over everything that we have so far.

"Charity is assaulted by Jenson Thomas back in August. Unbeknown to anyone, the assault was witnessed by Jenson's partner, Roxanne. Roxanne meets up with Charity a few days before the trial to say she is going to testify in court against Jenson. Roxanne then leaves Charity to order a taxi while she gets picked up by her secret lover, Terry Forshaw, and they drive to the woods for some hanky-panky in Terry's van. Afterwards, Roxanne was dropped close to her home, which she shares with Jenson, at five pm. Charity was last seen at the garden centre by Roxanne at four-twenty, and after checking with all the taxi ranks in the area, we know she didn't ring for one. Jenson says he arrived home from work at six-thirty that evening, where he and Roxanne stayed all night together. One of them is lying because Roxanne stated he didn't arrive home until after midnight. Terry Forshaw was seen driving to meet Roxanne on Friday afternoon but there is no CCTV of him and Roxanne leaving the garden centre together as she claimed. Roxanne had turned her mobile phone off so they wouldn't be disturbed, so tech can't even track her movements. However, on checking Terry's phone, luckily for us, he had a fitness tracker, which shows his phone was in a lay-by not far from Barton Grange from four to four-thirty pm on Friday. The phone is then switched off until it wakes up again at eighteen minutes past six at this location here." Lizzie pointed to an area on Google Maps that showed a remote area by water.

"That's Stocks reservoir, boss! Do you think he could've killed Charity? He was a builder so could easily have access to bricks and that." Dovey was excited at the prospect of discovering this new information.

"Not if Roxanne Clarke is telling the truth. I mean, there is a large, wooded area nearby. Unfortunately, Terry's phone gets turned off again so we don't know where he went from here and we can't ask him now, can we? However, his van has been searched and if there is any trace of Charity having been in that van, forensics will find it. I'm still waiting on the results. We do know that he went back home to Leyland though sometime after leaving the campsite with his wife Emma on Saturday afternoon. She said they arrived home at five-ish, and after unpacking the camping stuff, they watched TV in bed. Emma has also admitted lying to us about arriving at the campsite with Terry; she caught the train from Preston by herself and he only collected her from the train station at nine am on Saturday morning.

"Terry's murder was reported by Emma at two-forty-five this afternoon when she got back from shopping to find him bloody and beaten on the kitchen floor. Neighbours reported seeing Terry invite a heavily-built man into the house at about one pm and he left just before two. Unfortunately, the man wore a baseball cap so we have no real description of his face from the neighbours or clear images from their security cameras. The man left on foot, heading towards a local park, and then there are no more sightings. Forensics have been all over the Forshaw's house today so fingers crossed they find something. Emma Forshaw can be seen on camera shopping in Asda at the time of Terry's murder, so she can be ruled out as a suspect."

"Could Emma have found out about the affair and hired someone to kill Terry, ma'am?"

"We looked into that and their financial records show a mountain of debt. She couldn't afford to pay a hitman. There is nothing to make us think Emma is involved, but I like your quick-thinking, Verity. You will make a good detective one day."

The young constable was beaming with pride from the DI's praise.

"Verity, take some officers first thing and check out that area where Terry's phone was last picked up. Let me know if you find anything significant. Dovey, you will attend the search of Jenson's properties while I give the press conference with Lorna Fitzpatrick. If you find anything that links Jenson to the murders, arrest the bugger.

"Right, I think that's about it for now. I need to nip home for a shower and to cover my eyebags! I can't go on telly looking like this."

Lizzie was beginning to feel her age as her two young colleagues still looked fresh and awake at this ungodly hour.

The bright winter sun was just rising as Lizzie patted the thick concealer under her tired eyes and the comfortable double bed behind her seemed to be calling her name. Dressing quickly in her best grey suit and crisp, white shirt, she gave herself the once-over in the mirror.

"You'll do," she said to her reflection, and headed back out to work.

The press conference was a sea of faces, cameras and questions. Poor Lorna Fitzpatrick had held herself together well, and her tearful appeal would surely prick someone's conscience to come forward. Feeling positive, Lizzie went to update the DCI over a very strong coffee while they waited for DS Dove to return.

"After a thorough search of the fly-fishery, café and Mr Thomas's home address and vehicle, a bag matching Charity Fitzpatrick's was found hidden under the footwell of his car. The bag also contained Charity's mobile phone. Texts arranging to meet Roxanne Clarke were found on the phone, confirming Roxanne's statement. Thomas has been arrested on suspicion of Charity's murder and is being brought in as we speak, sir. Constable Harris has taken a team to the area where our other victim Terry Forshaw's mobile was last used. That phone is now missing. CSI has found tyre tracks that match Terry's van there, plus two sets of footprints. The most promising evidence is the rowboat found hidden in thick brambles; I believe this is where Charity was brought to die. We know that Terry and Jenson were mates. They could've killed her together so she couldn't testify in court. However, Terry was sleeping with Roxanne Clarke who is Thomas's fiancé. Perhaps he also killed Terry in revenge."

Jenson Thomas was all lawyered up, and he sat arrogantly opposite Lizzie and Dovey in the interview room. The afternoon was growing late and the dark sky outside the small window made the fluorescent lights of the room seem overly bright.

"I've told you over and over, I have no idea how Charity's bag and phone ended up in my car! I haven't seen that bitch since she accused me of assault."

"You still seem to have a lot of anger, Mr Thomas. Charity's testimony could've seen you sent to jail and ruined your business and your reputation, not to mention your pending marriage. It's rather convenient, don't you think, that Charity was killed just before the trial? Also, Roxanne has told us that you didn't arrive home on the night of the murder until after midnight. You lied to us about your whereabouts. Why did you do that, Mr Thomas? Was it because you were at the reservoir with Terry Forshaw? Did he help you to murder Charity and then you had him killed too because he was having an affair with your fiancé?"

This was Lizzie at her best. Throwing herself in head first, she didn't give the suspect chance to think up a lie before firing the next question at him.

"What the hell are you talking about? Terry's dead? I didn't even know that, and as for Roxanne, she would never…!"

"Mr Thomas, you are connected to both victims and we have enough to charge you. I think it's about time you start telling us the truth, don't you?"

Dovey got in on the act now and he felt they were close to a confession.

After a whispered discussion with his lawyer, the suspect told them how he received an anonymous text informing him of Roxie's affair with Terry. So, he had one of his men spy on Roxie, who saw them both together on numerous occasions. On the night of Charity's murder, Jenson met up with the man, who showed him the video evidence. Angered and humiliated, Jenson ordered this man to give Terry a good beating and warn him to stay away from Roxanne.

"I only said to teach Terry a lesson, I swear. I didn't know he'd killed him! His name is Robert Haig and he can vouch for where I was that night. We were at his caravan until almost one in the morning, drinking and going over stuff."

Lizzie nodded at Dovey, who then left the room. Lizzie stated this for the tape and suspended the interview.

It had been another hectic day, but Lizzie believed they were gaining ground with the investigation. Robert Haig had been arrested for the manslaughter of Terry Forshaw and it was up to the CPS if it went to court. Haig confirmed Jenson's version of events, proving that Jenson wasn't the person with Terry when Charity was murdered.

Lizzie was still puzzled about the bag and phone found in his car though. Climbing into bed with a sigh, she felt exhausted but also fidgety. Twirling the two plain gold rings that hung on a chain around her pale neck, Lizzie flicked through old photos on her mobile phone; David's handsome, rugged face smiled back at her from the small screen. God, she still missed him so much. There had never been anyone else since, and there never would be. David was the love of her life and she wasn't interested in replacing him. They had been very happy, and you don't get lucky like that twice.

The loud and unexpected ring of the house phone made her jump. No one ever called her on the landline; it was only there for the broadband. Picking up the receiver, Lizzie assumed it would be a wrong number.

"Hello," she said, feeling strange speaking on such an outdated handset.

The breathing on the other end of the line was quiet, but there was definitely someone there, listening.

"Hello?" Lizzie repeated. "Who is this?" Then the line went dead.

Quickly, she dialled 1471 but the number was withheld. Any chance of her sleeping now was out of the question.

Lizzie had seen almost every hour of the slowly passing night. Outside, the birds began to sing, announcing the start of a new day. As she perched on a stool in the kitchen with both hands hugging a very strong cup of Colombian, Lizzie stared at the wall in a trance. The investigation was puzzling for sure, but at least they had some solid leads now. The strange things that had been happening to Lizzie at home though were disturbing her now. The man in the garden, the letter, and now the funny phone call. She was being targeted by someone. Lizzie wondered if some long-lost relative of Roy Peters had sought her out for revenge, or perhaps someone with a grudge had found out about her past and was trying to frighten her. She decided she would swallow her pride and inform her colleagues at the station of what had happened before things escalated.

7

FEELING LIKE A ZOMBIE, LIZZIE walked into the station and sat down heavily at her desk. Verity came bouncing into the room like Tigger.

"Morning ma'am. Oh, you look done in, boss. Is everything alright?"

"Morning Constable, thanks for that. I'm fine; nothing a good night's sleep won't fix. Where are we at with all the forensics?

"Sorry, ma'am, I didn't mean you looked awful, just tired."

"Stop digging yourself in deeper, Verity. Here, boss, I thought you might appreciate this." Dovey walked in and placed a fresh coffee and a Danish pastry in front of Lizzie.

"Thanks, Andy, you're a star."

Verity shot him a dark look and whispered "arsehole" under her breath.

"The forensics, Verity?" Lizzie didn't have the patience for these two right now.

"Yes, ma'am, sorry. Terry Forshaw's van had been thoroughly cleaned so we didn't find anything. DNA in his house proved that Jenson's henchman was there but nothing to place Charity there; however, rope matching the one used to restrain her was found hidden in a steel barrel in the Forshaw's back garden. Terry was probably going to burn it.

"Now, the area where we found the boat is much more interesting, boss. One set of footprints from the scene was from a pair of size five wellington boots and the other set from some heavy-duty type of work boots, size ten. The tread and size of the work boots match those found in Terry's garage. The welly prints, although the wellies had been cleaned, were a match for the pair found in the back of his work van. Tyre tracks leading to and from the scene have been confirmed as coming from that van too. Both sets of boots had minute traces of mud and foliage. Charity's DNA was found ingrained in the wood on one side of the hidden boat, and a small hair was discovered trapped in the rim of an oar. The full report should've been sent to your e-mail by now."

"So, we can more or less say for certain that Terry Forshaw was the one who murdered Charity, but who was with him? We know it wasn't Jenson. The wellies belonged to Terry's wife, Emma, but she was still at home in Leyland at the time of the murder. Verity, check that out again. Check the CCTV of the railway station; we need evidence of her boarding that train."

The caffeine and sugar lifted Lizzie's energy levels as she read over the forensics report. Absentmindedly pulling at the skin of her lower lip, Lizzie pondered the evidence before her. We know Terry killed Charity. We know Robert Haig killed Terry at Jenson's bidding. Something wasn't right, Lizzie could feel it in her stomach. They were missing a piece of the puzzle. Scrolling further down the report, Lizzie dropped the pastry as she re-read the final paragraph and then ran from her desk.

"Dovey! Come with me now!"

Lizzie and Dovey sped down the motorway, followed by a team of uniformed officers, blues and twos demanding urgency.

"There's no answer, ma'am. Emma Forshaw isn't picking up," Dovey stated anxiously.

"Keep trying, Andy, I just hope we're not too late."

As usual, Lizzie was the first to run through the open front door and into the Forshaws' front room.

Dovey and the other officers were right behind her though.

"Put the knife down and we can talk about this. Emma doesn't know anything." Lizzie spoke calmly and held a hand up, instructing the others to stay back.

Emma was being held by the scruff of her jumper with a kitchen knife at her throat, a look of sheer terror in her wide eyes.

"How did you figure out it was me? I was so sure I'd covered my tracks."

"You did. You nearly had us all fooled with your crocodile tears. But one tiny piece of evidence got you caught; a single hair was your downfall. That short strand of hair coloured with cherry-red dye proved you were in the boat with Charity. You were very clever though, Roxanne, how you set them all up."

Lizzie had figured it all out as soon as she realised who the hair belonged to. "You made sure we could identify you as the friend who met Charity at the garden centre. You wanted to be brought in to tell us about Jenson's fake alibi and the affair with Terry."

"Men, they're so easy to manipulate. Terry was like putty in my hands. I seduced him for weeks before, until I knew that he'd do anything for me. I convinced him to help me kill Charity and explained how we could blame Jenson, getting rid of him so we could be together. Well, that's what Terry thought.

"After the meeting at Barton Grange, I offered her a lift home with my new boyfriend. Once she was in the van, Terry knocked her out cold with one punch and we drove her to the reservoir. The boat had been bought second-hand ages ago and he paid cash for it so the purchase couldn't be traced. While tying the bricks to Charity, she began to wake up. She was in a right panic and started to scream, so Terry had to put tape over her mouth. I just laughed in her face, the stupid little, rich bitch wasn't so high and mighty anymore. Terry had to hold her while I rowed the boat using my head torch to see by. Charity was wriggling ironically like a fish out of water, then splash; we rolled her over the side and down she sank. Then silence. No more Charity."

Roxanne was still holding the knife against Emma as she boasted about her sickening plan.

"But why not just kill Jenson?" Lizzie asked

"Because killing Charity was payback for her ruining my life. Me and Jenson had been happy until she led him on. We were going to get married and start a family. I could never feel the same about him after that. I would lie awake for hours plotting my revenge. Being sent to prison would hurt Jenson more than killing him. There are a few people in jail who would like to settle some old scores with him."

"But once Terry had served his purpose, he also had to go, didn't he, Roxanne?" Lizzie was trying to keep her talking while Dovey crept in through the back door.

"Terry was a drunken idiot but I admit, I had a bit of a soft spot for him. Even so, he was a witness and I couldn't risk him blurting out what we'd done after a few too many beers. I knew Jenson would be furious once he found out about our affair, so I bought a cheap pay-as-you-go mobile phone and sent him a text pretending to be a concerned friend. I didn't have to kill Terry; Jenson would do that for me. That just left little Emma here… she swears Terry didn't tell her anything, but why take the risk? And I'm going to jail now anyway so I may as well finish the job."

Emma let out a piercing scream as Roxanne pressed the knife harder into her skin, but DS Dove suddenly leapt at the crazed woman, knocking her to the floor. Lizzie rushed to kick the fallen knife out of reach and then helped her sergeant, who was still wrestling with Roxanne, who was kicking and screaming like a banshee.

Uniformed officers helped the badly-shaken but unharmed victim to the ambulance while Roxanne Clarke was arrested and taken into custody.

"Well done, everyone, cheers!" DCI Piper had treated the team to a celebratory drink in the local pub.

"Cheers, sir!"

Taking a large gulp of his pint, Dovey checked his watch.

"Just this one for me, boss. I've hardly seen Keeley and the little one for days. I'm taking them to a Christmas market tomorrow."

"You've earned a few days off, Andy. Go and enjoy some quality time with the family. Thanks for doing a great job. If you hadn't stopped Roxanne when you did, Emma might not have survived."

"Ahh, it was nothing, ma'am. All in a day's work for us heroes." Dovey laughed and Verity gave him a friendly punch in the arm.

"And thanks for all your hard work as well, Verity. I'll be putting in a good word for you with the big man."

Lizzie meant it. She was lucky to be sharing the job with a team that she could rely on; a team who were beginning to feel like a family. As she stood surrounded by the people she trusted, Sabine, the pathologist, came over.

"Hi Lizzie, well done on getting justice for our victim. She can finally rest in peace now. Did you get that message from the lab? I sent it to your personal e-mail as you asked. We found some DNA on the seal of that envelope you gave us."

"Oh no, I've been so wrapped up in paperwork and everything, I've not had time to check. Thanks, Sabine, I appreciate your discretion."

Pushing through the old, revolving door of the pub, Lizzie stepped out into the icy evening air. It was freezing and her fingers were struggling to find the e-mail on her phone. On opening the file, all the surrounding music and chatter from the pub seemed to stop and the floor swirled before Lizzie's eyes. She read the words again and again. This couldn't be possible. The DNA found on the envelope belonged to David Holland, her dead husband.